BOUND ON EARTH

BOUND ON EARTH

The Sacred Feminine
Unfolding

A Novel

Judith G. Hunter & Mary Ann Eaton

iUniverse, Inc.
New York Bloomington Shanghai

BOUND ON EARTH
The Sacred Feminine Unfolding

Copyright © 2008 by Judith G. Hunter & Mary Ann Eaton

All rights reserved. No part of this book may be used or reproduced by any means, graphic, electronic, or mechanical, including photocopying, recording, taping or by any information storage retrieval system without the written permission of the publisher except in the case of brief quotations embodied in critical articles and reviews.

iUniverse books may be ordered through booksellers or by contacting:

iUniverse
1663 Liberty Drive
Bloomington, IN 47403
www.iuniverse.com
1-800-Authors (1-800-288-4677)

Because of the dynamic nature of the Internet, any Web addresses or links contained in this book may have changed since publication and may no longer be valid.

This is a work of fiction. All of the characters, names, incidents, organizations, and dialogue in this novel are either the products of the author's imagination or are used fictitiously.

ISBN: 978-0-595-49095-0 (pbk)
ISBN: 978-0-595-60967-3 (ebk)

Printed in the United States of America

Prologue

"Generation to generation, down through the centuries, this legend has survived in the oral tradition. Each time the story is told, it has been the responsibility of the family matriarch to determine when and to whom this sacred legend would be revealed. As Keeper of the Knowledge, and its guardian, she only entrusts the story with the first-born female of a first-born female, thereby ensuring its sacred truth. Each new Keeper of the Knowledge in turn preserves and protects the story as those who have gone before her. I am a Keeper of the Knowledge. At the age of seventy, I have held this legend dear to my heart for forty-two years waiting to pass it on. So why have I decided to break from tradition and put these sacred words on paper now?

Centuries have passed from the first telling, and those whom the story protected have long since passed on. Our family is small now with the only other surviving member being my granddaughter. She is a first-born, and as tradition dictates, she will be the next Keeper of the Knowledge.

In my heart of hearts, I believe the danger existing in the ancient legend is not a threat to my granddaughter or me. Centuries of time have provided a safety net. Yet, the ancient story needs to be told, so that we may always remember. It is a beautiful story of love and hope for all humanity. So with much thought and prayer, I have also chosen to make you, the reader, a Keeper of the Knowledge, entrusting you to cherish it for eternity."

Rachel

... and so begins Rachel's book, and the disclosure of an ancient prophecy that will uproot the basic beliefs of religions throughout the world.

Chapter 1

Mariah's scream echoed in the night, as she awoke with a frightening jolt. She sat up in her bed sobbing, whispering, "Joe … Oh … Joe." It was the same nightmare about her husband she had been having every night. He was calling out to her for help in the midst of gunfire and bombing, but she couldn't get to him. There was always a tremendous explosion that would startle her awake.

She wiped her tears, as she got up to change her perspiration-drenched nightgown. The light was already on because she dreaded the dark. It only brought sleepless nights, or short bouts of terror-filled sleep. Mariah caught a glimpse of herself in the mirror. The reflection was that of a stranger. She stared for a moment, searching for a flicker of recognition, but empty eyes returned her stare. There were dark circles under her even darker almond shaped eyes, the same eyes he had kissed gently when he told her she was beautiful. She felt the tears threaten to overflow again and quickly turned from the mirror. She pulled her thick brown hair back clipping it with a barrette. It didn't matter what she looked like anymore. She sighed deeply. It simply didn't matter. Nothing mattered.

As she climbed back into bed, she felt sick. The lump in her throat never seemed to go away, and once again she wondered if she could actually die from a broken heart. It certainly felt like she could. In her darkest moments she even imagined death might be a welcome release from the weight of her grief.

The soft colors of morning were slowly brightening the sky, as Rachel carried a tray with a pot of tea and warm blueberry muffins out to the sun porch. Her granddaughter sat there silently gazing at the glistening waves, breaking gently on the shore. It would be another beautiful sunny day, and a gentle sea breeze already filled the room with the sweet fragrance of beach plum roses. Mariah was snuggled deep into the old wicker chair. The overstuffed floral cushions seemed to be warmly hugging her. She appeared childlike with her dark pink robe pulled tightly around her petite frame. She was no longer the vibrant outspoken young woman Rachel loved to see rise to any challenge. She seemed like a stranger, living in her own private world, since the tragic incident with poor Joe. Yet as bad as Rachel felt, she knew better than to try to force her way into that world. She certainly understood the pain Mariah was feeling, having experienced similar grief in her own life. Still, it didn't make it any easier to watch her beloved grandchild suffering.

Nevertheless, seventy years of accumulated wisdom had taught her much. She realized Mariah must sort out this devastating loss and accept her husband's fate before she could begin to heal.

Sitting down, she poured them each a cup of tea. The grief-stricken young woman picked up the china cup and staring out at the roses sadly asked, "Why me? Why Joe? Why Grand, why?"

"Grand" was an endearing name Mariah had started calling her as a child, it always made Rachel feel exceptional. She sipped her tea slowly, pondering these fragile questions.

"My dear child, these are not really questions we can answer. I have always trusted there are reasons for everything that occurs in this world. But, I also believe we will not fully understand why these events happen until we reach the next life. I realize this is a dreadful time for you, but you must try to stop tormenting yourself with questions no one can answer." Her eyes filled with tears of sympathy as she spoke.

"It's just so hard, Grand. I can't stop thinking about Joe being tortured, and how much he suffered before, before …" Mariah burst into tears, she reached for the tissues on the wicker table beside her. After a few minutes, she managed to regain her composure by breathing deeply. Her gaze was drawn back to the vast ocean, she continued speaking softly, still sniffling.

"I know they say he died for all of us, for what he believed in. And I do know that's true." She stopped to take another deep breath. "But why did they have to torture and humiliate him before they killed him?"

They were both silent for a time. A gull gave out a mournful cry overhead, as if he had been listening and agreed with Mariah. She stood, walking to the window, "Joe always tried to live in harmony with the world. He liked everyone, he brought joy to people's lives, he made them laugh and forget their troubles. He truly believed by going to Iraq he could help bring peace to the world, through this same approach, with kindness and harmony. Yet, look what they did to him, it's just not fair. How can I not be consumed with hatred for people who would perform such atrocities on a beautiful loving soul like my Joe?"

Rachel cleared her throat, as she moved her rocking chair closer to Mariah, gently touching her arm.

"You know sweetie, everything you are saying is true, but try not to let your heart harden. Becoming bitter will only hurt you, and it will not change anything." She looked at her granddaughter compassionately. "Please believe me when I tell you love is stronger than death. I know."

She hesitated, the only noises were the waves breaking on the near by shore and the distant cry of a gull. She spoke slowly, "Women in our family have faced similar ordeals down through time."

Once again Rachel silently hesitated, as she weighed the validity and timing of what she was about to say.

"There is a long ago story, which was told to my grandmother by her grandmother and so on back through our ancestry. I believe the time has come for me to pass it on to you." She unconsciously fingered the pendant she wore.

She looked thoughtfully at her granddaughter. Mariah was of course puzzled and started to speak, but Grand held up her hand stopping her. She proceeded slowly, choosing her words carefully. "I'll answer what questions I can when I'm finished. I do not want to forget any details you should know." She watched the waves for a moment.

"With the passing of this legend to a new generation, also comes a forewarning to always keep this story in oral form. Supposedly, to do otherwise will invite some mysterious retribution, but I think that's ludicrous, so after my retirement I decided to write down our family legend. I am now in the process of writing the book, and I feel it is important I share the story with you before it is published. I didn't want you to think I was a crazy old woman. That's why I've been waiting for the right time to tell you. Sadly, I believe Joe's death has made this the right time. I would like to read to you from my manuscript, so you will know the complete story, as I write it." Rachel picked up her laptop and began to read slowly.

Chapter 2

It had been a long day and the young widow was exhausted. She had buried her husband only a few hours earlier, and her head was throbbing from the memories. Family and friends surrounded her, but all she wanted was some quiet time.

She found her younger sister and told her that she was going to lie down for a while. "My head hurts, and I need a quiet place," she said as she massaged her temples.

"I'll check on you later. I'm sure people will be leaving shortly, especially when they know you have gone to rest," Ruth told her gently.

"Thank you," was the reply from the woman already heading in the direction of her bedroom.

Once behind the closed door of her room, the woman let out a weary sigh. She crossed the sparsely furnished room to a table that held a water pitcher. She poured the cool liquid into the empty bowl and started to wash her face and neck. Feeling more refreshed, she lay back on her bed and closed her eyes. Although she was tired, she did not fall asleep. Her thoughts went back to the day before. Surrounded by some friends, her husband had been in the garden contemplating the events of the past week. Soldiers arrived at the back gate and grabbed him. His nearby friends tried to rescue him, but the soldiers were armed. Soon the small crowd backed down, freeing the soldiers to take the gentle man into custody. His family and friends followed at a safe distance.

He was quickly taken to a nearby court manned by local officials, politicians, and even a few religious men. It was not long before a crowd gathered. Some were angered this arrest had taken place. Others chanted, "Find him guilty."

The arrested man stood tall with his hands tied in front of him, his garment soiled and torn. He remained silent in front of his captors. Why had he been arrested? He had done nothing wrong. In his silence, he had tried to hear what the officials were discussing, but he was not near enough. Yet, he was able to determine by their body language that there was disagreement among them.

When he turned his head to the left, along with armed soldiers, he could see his friends and family on the edge of the crowd. They looked helpless and worried, especially his wife. For a few moments, the couple's eyes met. She looked scared and his heart ached for her. Suddenly, the crowd grew louder, and his thoughts quickly returned to the moment at hand. Upon orders, a young soldier stepped forward carrying a whip, just as another soldier violently stripped the arrested man of his robe. A cracking sound could be heard throughout the crowd as the leather strip tore into his flesh. Again and again the soldier skillfully wielded the whip, and soon the back of the young man was bloody with numerous slashes. As the blood dripped to the ground the crowd chanted louder, "Kill him!"

For a moment, the officials interrupted the whipping to ask the young man a question. His answer could not be heard, but the whip could again be seen making contact with his already raw skin. The officials obviously did not like the response the softly spoken man had given.

"Kill him, kill him," the crowds shouted.

The torture continued, seeming endless, with the soldier only pausing when an official asked another question. Each time the official walked away with a disgusted look on his face, and each time the whip continued to make contact with the accused man's torn and bloody body.

Eventually the beaten man was dragged through the city streets to the hanging place. "Kill him, kill him," the mobs chanted.

His wife watched as she sobbingly whispered, "My Lord, my Lord." But he did not respond, he had heaved his last breath. He was dead.

"Noooo." The young woman screamed, as a nearby soldier mercilessly rammed a sword into her husband's already limp body. "No, no, no," she whimpered as she sank to the ground.

Her husband's friend, Joseph, gently raised her to her feet, still sobbing. "Come, we must ask the officials to bury your husband. We cannot dishonor him. Soon it will be sundown, and the Sabbath will be upon us. Hurry."

When permission was given, and the dead body was safely in the arms of friends, Joseph led the small party to his own nearby estate. He had offered to bury his friend in his own gardens, and the family graciously accepted.

When the body had been prepared and prayers said, a boulder was pushed against the grave opening. Her beloved was gone from her forever.

Now, alone in her room, she did not know how she would go on without her husband by her side. They had traveled the countryside together, working alongside him as he preached to ever-growing crowds. Could she continue his work as he had asked? There were so many unanswered questions stirring inside her. Right now she was overwhelmed and needed time to sort through all that had happened to find her answers. Eventually she drifted off to sleep, leaving her thoughts and sorrows for another day.

Chapter 3

Rachel saw the tears slipping silently down her granddaughter's cheeks and decided that was enough. She closed her computer, gently patting Mariah's leg, as she got up from her chair.

"You go lie down for a bit, honey. We have a busy week ahead of us."

"But, Grand, I want to know more of the story."

"There is plenty of time for that later. It is a long complicated story. As I pass it on to you, I want to get the details right. And you have much to think about already. Now go rest, you are too pale."

She kissed her on the cheek, taking the teacup from her. Mariah rose from the chair obediently going to her room. Grand was right. She felt like her mind was a jumble of endless thoughts, as her eyes became heavy.

Her room had not changed since the day she had moved out. The beautiful fluffy comforter with an old-fashioned rose print and lace edging still covered the four-poster mahogany bed, which had also been her mother's as a child. She felt close to her mother knowing she had slept in this same bed. When she was a child her parents were killed in a plane crash. Her maternal grandmother had not hesitated to adopt her and raise her as her own. It had been a terribly sad time for the both of them. That was when Mariah had started calling her Grand because to even say the word mother in grandmother had made her cry. Now, as she slipped under the soft comforter, she felt like she was home again. Closing her eyes, thoughts of Joe drifted into her mind. Suddenly, her grief grabbed her hard. She muffled her sobs with the pillow, until finally falling asleep, praying not to dream.

Chapter 4

The world seemed to being moving at a different pace than Mariah these past couple weeks. She stared at the black dress hanging on the closet door, her funeral dress. It felt like months since she had received the call that Joe's plane had been shot down. From that point on life had gone into slow motion, time itself became meaningless. Then there had been the pictures on television, which brought her to her knees, begging for God's help. There was Joe blindfolded, obviously hurt and abused, stating he was a Captain in the United States Air Force. His masked captors held a saber to his throat, while instructing him to beg for his life. When Joe stayed silent, refusing to bend to his captors, Mariah quickly realized she would never be in his arms again.

It was all so strange when the Air Force representatives came to the door to tell her he was dead. Of course, intuitively she had already known, but to hear someone actually confirm it felt like she had been stabbed in the heart. She let out a wail, which could only come from the depths of grief. The officers had helped her to the sofa and called her grandmother. She kept quietly explaining to them that her husband could not be dead because she loved him, as though her love could change the reality of what they had confirmed. When Grand arrived they left. She sobbed in her grandmother's arms for what must have been hours, then Grand packed her things and took her home.

The news media was relentless. They called for interviews and even knocked on the front door. But Grand never lost her composure, always shielding her granddaughter.

Mariah's pain was personal, so private she hadn't even considered it would be of interest to the public. She refused to talk to any of the media, so eventually they stopped using her name. They simply referred to her as his widow. And what a foreign word widow was for a twenty-seven-year-old. The label and age just didn't fit together. Yet, here she was preparing for her husband's funeral, now that his body had been brought home.

It felt like it had taken forever until Joe's remains had been recovered and brought home to the United States. Mariah felt like she was in some kind of limbo, with one day running into the next until she was drained of any true conception of time. There was only the before and after of Joe's death.

Grand and Mariah had been there to meet him when they carried the flag-draped coffin off the plane. Mariah had dressed carefully, taking extra time with her make-up and hair. She wanted to look especially pretty for Joe on that day. She wore a fitted peach colored linen dress, which enhanced her petite figure and dark complexion. It was one of his favorites. Her chestnut hair was pulled back in a French braid, and the only jewelry she wore was a gold cross with entwined wedding rings on it. Joe had given it to her on their wedding day. There was a simple beauty about her, which showed her love for her husband.

Holding Grand's hand tightly, as the military men escorted the coffin from the plane she forced herself not to cry in public. Joe would have told her to be strong, and she wanted him to be proud of her. She truly believed he was with her in spirit.

The first to approach them was the Chaplain, introducing himself as Michael Santini. He was a heavyset nervous man, with terrible body odor, and breath smelling of garlic. Taking Mariah's hand in his left hand and Rachel's in his right, he said how sorry he was for their loss, and asked them to bow their heads in prayer for Joe. Rachel felt very uncomfortable with his sweaty touch and shaky hand. He definitely held onto both of their hands for a little too long. Telling them he would come to visit them before the funeral he handed Mariah his card, in case she needed to talk. Rachel looked directly into the Chaplain's eyes as she thanked him. Although he tried to act kind, she felt the man was insincere. Her intuition warned her he was not to be trusted.

The Chaplain stepped aside, as there was another airman waiting behind him. The next man in line stammered as he said his name was Peter, that Joe was a really good guy, and that he was terribly sorry for her loss. He fidgeted, moving from one foot to the other, as he stared at Mariah. Finally, gingerly taking her hand, he explained that he knew everything about her from her husband. It seemed innocent enough at first, but then he touched her hair telling her she was even more beautiful than he imagined. Rachel was speaking with another person and didn't notice her granddaughter recoil from the peculiar man. Luckily, at that moment, a tall young officer approached to introduce himself, saying nothing Peter quickly walked away.

Unaware of the strange scene he had inadvertently disrupted, the handsome officer smiled politely removing his hat. "My name is John Benson, please let me offer my condolences for the loss of your husband. Joe was a very special person. We flew together and became good friends during his first tour of duty. I was honored to escort him home."

"Thank you, John," was all Mariah could manage to say. Pale and shaking she felt her knees begin to give out, and the next thing she knew she heard Grand's voice distantly calling her name. She could not understand who was holding her and for a moment thought it was Joe. She forced her eyes open to see Grand's very worried face close to her own.

"Honey, you fainted. Just be still for a minute. Thank heavens John caught you, or you could have hurt yourself!"

Mariah looked up to see the attractive officer sitting on the pavement, her head was resting in his arms. Slowly she realized what had happened, there was a curious crowd around her. Feeling quite embarrassed she tried to get up, but they wouldn't let her. Still feeling a bit woozy, she closed her eyes. Finally they helped her to her feet, then slowly to the waiting car. John asked if he could call later to see how she was. Grand nodded thanking him for his help.

"Mariah, I am calling the doctor when we get home. You have been under a tremendous strain with all you have to deal with. I think it would be wise to simply have a check-up."

She sat with her head back, eyes closed. She was too weak to argue and didn't totally disagree anyway.

Chapter 5

Rachel listened to the messages once she had Mariah settled in bed. She was so concerned about her granddaughter's health she was only half listening, until a man's voice caught her attention. He was talking very low, so she replayed the message. The voice whispered, "I know … I know she's there … I know."

An icy wave rolled over her, she felt chilled to the core by the stranger's voice. It sounded like someone she had heard before. She played the message over and listened closely, but couldn't place the voice. She didn't understand his message, but it felt threatening. The doorbell rang at that moment, startling her. She could see a florist's truck in the driveway as she walked through the living room to open the front door. The delivery boy was holding a dozen yellow long stemmed roses arranged in a beautiful crystal vase. She thanked him and placed the arrangement on the antique sideboard, right inside the door. The card had Mariah's name on it, though curious, she left it next to the ever-growing pile of unopened cards that had been arriving daily. The phone rang right then, and with a bit of apprehension she hurried back to the kitchen to get it. She was relieved to hear the voice of her literary agent.

Joan Hale attempted to be polite, inquiring about Mariah and how everything was going, but Rachel knew a call from her was always about business. She was an aggressive New York agent, and everything with her was about the bottom line. Certainly, having a posh Fifth Avenue office, driving a big Mercedes when she was not in a limo, and spending weekends in the Hamptons required a substantial income. Consequently, this agent did not lift a finger unless it was financially beneficial for her. She idolized money and saw no shame in admitting it.

Joan tried hard to sound sincere saying, "I feel terrible bothering you at a time like this. But, I was wondering if you might have anything new on the book to show me when I come down for the funeral?"

"Yes, Joan, ironically this whole sad situation seems to have the legend very much on my mind. I'll try to get more writing done before you arrive. It has not been easy to find the time with taking care of my granddaughter and trying to make the arrangements," she sighed deeply.

"Oh, I fully understand, Hon. I wouldn't even have considered asking you at a time like this, except I have a couple big publishers hot on the subject just from the synopsis you wrote, and we could really benefit from getting a bidding war going! If you get my drift?"

Rachel smiled. "Yes, I get your drift. I'll see what I can get done before you come." It was always about the money with her, but then that was what made her one of the top literary agents in New York City.

She decided to try to get some writing done while Mariah rested. The doctor had said he could not get there for a couple hours anyway. Now sitting in her study with the blank computer screen glaring back at her, she stared out at the ocean thinking about the day's events, daydreaming more than contemplating her writing. Yet, when she finally turned her attention to the keyboard the words seemed to flow from her fingertips. Writing had always been therapeutic for her, and this particular writing was the most important of her life. Her imagination soared back in time, as her fingers danced on the keyboard, literally taking on a life of their own.

"The hot sun was high in the sky when Mary ..."

Chapter 6

The hot sun was high in the sky when Mary awoke the next day. Streams of sunlight warmed the already oppressive air in her room. As she stretched the stiffness from her body, she couldn't believe she had slept so late into the day. She squinted as she glanced toward the sunlit window wondering how late it was.

She sat up and swung her feet to the floor. Suddenly all the horrid memories of the day before came rushing back. Her head began to pound and her stomach became queasy. Tears slipped from her dark brown eyes, and in a moment she was bent over sobbing uncontrollably.

From the next room, Mary's sister heard the crying and quickly opened the bedroom door. She ran to her sister's side and cradled her in her arms. Each clung to the other for comfort and support. It was a sad time in each of their lives. After what seemed to be an eternity, the sobs diminished to whimpers, and eventually Mary could cry no more.

"What am I going to do? I miss him so," she said in a low voice. "Why did they kill him? What did he ever do to them?"

"I don't know. I just don't know," whispered her sister. "Come Mary. Why don't you wash up and change your clothes, you'll feel better. I'll fix some food, you need to eat something."

Mary agreed. Still sitting at the edge of the bed, she took her long brown curly hair and twisted it into a knot on top of her head. Without thinking, she reached for a comb on a nearby table. Her fingers gently touched the cool ivory teeth of the comb. It had been a gift from her husband. She had treasured the beautiful gift and wore it often. Slowly she stroked the smooth surface as though she was lovingly stroking his face.

For just a moment she smiled as she remembered how he loved to remove the comb and watch her hair tumble down her back. With eyes closed she let her curls fall from atop her head. She slowly ran her fingers through her hair, remembering the feel of his caress across the back of her head. His warm gentle fingers would continue down the front of her neck to the top of her breast. She sighed deeply as she felt every memory and recalled how her body responded to his loving touch. A single tear ran down her face at the realization those intimate moments would be no more.

Mary quickly re-knotted her hair and anchored it with the comb. She crossed the room to the dressing table where she washed the dusty grime from her body, and along with it her weary image. Feeling refreshed, she slipped into a pale blue robe and went to join her sister in the kitchen.

As she entered the doorway to the kitchen, Mary stopped to watch her sister bent over the hearth. This was Ruth's favorite room in the house, and the décor was warm and inviting, as well as functional. The room was well stocked with numerous pieces of pottery in a variety of sizes and shapes that she used to prepare the family meals. Dried herbs and fruits hung from wooden rafters over her worktable. Fresh flowers in earthen jars were placed on the window openings throughout the room. The hearth burned brightly, and a wonderful aroma rose from the cooking pot.

Ruth turned around as Mary moved to the center of the room. "Feeling better?"

"MMMM," she murmured as she approached the worktable.

Taking a bowl of meat and vegetables from her sister she moved to a stool in a corner of the room. Sitting down, she balanced the bowl on her lap trying to eat the prepared food. The aroma was wonderful, but the first taste was hard to swallow. Suddenly she had no appetite. Any attempt to continue eating produced a gagging reflex. Feeling as though she was going to be sick, she simply pushed the food around in the bowl, eventually putting it down on a nearby table.

Quietly Mary left the room heading outdoors to the garden. She aimlessly walked, shoulders drooping. Eventually she settled on a stone bench under one of the many fruit trees. The warm air was heavy with the sweet smell of their blossoms, closing her eyes she inhaled deeply of the fragrance.

"How am I going to survive without you by my side? Everywhere I look, I see your face. Memories are everywhere in this house, in this garden, in our room. I need you, please come back," she pleaded softly as her head gently rested on the tree behind her.

"Are you ill?" Ruth's words startled Mary. "You hardly ate any of your food."

"I'm sorry, Ruth, but I just couldn't eat. My heart is so heavy. I long for him. We had to bury him so quickly, I did not have a chance to say goodbye or tell him how much I love him and will miss him."

"You can go to the grave in the morning, once Sabbath has ended. I'll go with you if you want."

"No, I need to do this by myself." she said sorrowfully.

Ruth acknowledged her sister's request, seeing the grief on her older sister's face. She thought about how happy Mary and her husband had been. There had been great delight when each came into the other's presence, and their faces reflected their deep love. Alone now she seemed so small and frail.

They were a handsome couple. He was tall, and his lean body was tanned from constantly being outdoors. His dark brown hair hung loosely in waves about his face. When his full lips smiled, which was often, his large eyes seemed to sparkle with light. High cheekbones gave his face a chiseled look as though an artist had carved him from stone. But more than his good looks made him stand out in a crowd, people were drawn to his magnetic personality that was warm, gentle, and fun loving. He could be quite serious, but also quick with a hearty laugh.

Mary was beautiful, taller than most women in her village. Her height gave her a regal appearance, and she carried herself proudly. The sun-streaked wavy tresses on her head were her crowning glory, hanging well beneath her waist. She loved the feel of the wind in her hair and most of the time wore it loose. Many times, a double strand of pearls was tied as a band across her head, keeping away stray curls. This extraordinary appearance turned heads wherever she went. Her face was the color of cinnamon with soft pink cheeks and rose-colored lips that were pouty and sensual. When she spoke, though her voice was gentle, she commanded attention.

Together, side-by-side, they both had a promising future. They had been married less than a year, following a long friendship that budded into romance. They were meant for each other, and Mary was so pleased when her brother came to tell her his friend wanted her as his wife. The wedding took place only weeks after Mary had said yes.

The best wine from the family vineyards was served, but with many in attendance the urns had run dry. Mysteriously, after the groom checked the urns, the servants found them to be full again, saving the family from what could have been an embarrassing situation.

Ruth sighed deeply at the remembrance of happier days. She turned towards the house, and left her sister to her quiet thoughts. It would be hard, but hopefully time would heal her sister's wounded heart.

Chapter 7

Lost in her writing Rachel suddenly realized someone was alternately knocking on the front door and ringing the doorbell. She hurried from her study to find James at the door appearing very worried.

"Ah, Rachel my dear, you had me extremely concerned when you didn't answer the door." He bent down and kissed her on the cheek as he entered.

"I apologize, James. I was totally absorbed in my work."

He eyed her for a minute, as though trying to figure out what her work was. "Oh yes, the book you are writing, still won't tell me what it's about?"

She sensed the mischievous tone in his voice. He was an old dear friend, but always enjoyed teasing her. They had a long history together and were very close friends. She simply smiled at him.

"Mariah is in her bedroom laying down, come." She led the way upstairs, although he certainly knew his way through her house. He had become her doctor after her own husband died, and they had developed a gradual affection for each other through the years. Therefore, it had been natural for him to become Mariah's doctor when she came to live with her grandmother. The little girl had affectionately dubbed him Dr. James.

They heard stirring coming from the bedroom, as they approached. Rachel knocked on the door, announcing the doctor's arrival as she opened it. Mariah was sitting on the window seat with a picture album in her lap. It was she and Joe's wedding album. Her face was streaked with tears, she stood quickly, and James moved to give her a hug.

"I am so sorry Mariah, so very sorry." He hugged her warmly and then kissed her on the forehead.

She thanked him reaching for a tissue to wipe her face. He was slowly assessing her health by watching her. From the dark circles under her eyes and her hollowed cheeks, he suspected grief was robbing her of both sleep and appetite.

"I understand you had a fainting spell today."

"Yes, I really don't think it was any big deal."

He motioned for her to sit on the bed. "Well, let's check you out to be sure there's nothing wrong." He winked at her. "It will keep your grandmother happy."

James came downstairs to find Rachel in the kitchen preparing dinner. He explained that Mariah's grief was causing her stress and anxiety, which in turn was physically wearing her down. "I did take a blood and urine sample for tests, just as a precautionary measure. I'll call you if they show anything, but I am fairly sure they won't. Try to get her to eat little meals often. She might be able to get better nutrition that way. I offered her a sedative, but she refused. Call me if she changes her mind, or if you have any other concerns." Once again James kissed her gently on the cheek and said he'd show himself out.

He had no sooner left than the doorbell rang. Rachel assumed James had forgotten something, so she opened the door thinking it was him, but to her surprise, it was Chaplain Santini.

"Good afternoon, I hope I am not intruding. I did try to call, but your phone was busy. I thought I might speak with you and Mariah about Joe's funeral."

Rachel liked this man even less upon their second encounter. "I am terribly sorry you made the trip here for nothing, Chaplain. My granddaughter is sleeping, and I wouldn't presume to speak for her about such an important matter." She only had the door half open, having no intention of inviting him in. She pretended to be speaking quietly, so as not to disturb Mariah.

The Chaplain seemed to be perspiring excessively considering how cool the day had become. He nervously mobbed his brow with a hanky. "May I come back tomorrow? I will call first, of course."

"Please do call, and we will set up an appointment," Rachel replied rather coldly. He nodded, as she just about closed the door in his face.

Michael Santini wiped the sweat from the back of his thick neck and headed for his rental car thinking, *that's one tough old lady. She certainly is protective of the young widow.*

Mariah came down stairs asking who had been at the door. Grand told her it was the Chaplain, and also that she did not care for him.

"There is just something sneaky about him," she added returning to the kitchen.

Mariah spotted the yellow roses in the living room standing well above all the other arrangements friends had sent. It took her breath away for a moment because they were her favorite, and Joe was the only one who ever sent them to her. She went into parlor for a closer look and saw the card with her name on it. She let out a scream when she read it. The card read, *"Loving You Forever, J"*.

She shrieked, "Nooo!" hitting the roses, sending the vase and the other arrangements flying in every direction.

Rachel ran into the room just as her granddaughter collapsed sobbing onto the floor.

"How could anyone be so cruel? I just don't understand, Grand."

"I don't know, sweetie," Rachel replied as she read the card. "I just don't know." It grew dark in the living room, as she rocked her devastated granddaughter in her arms until the sobbing subsided. "Come sit in the kitchen, I'll clean this up later."

She sat at the table staring into her tea, while Grand talked to Dr. James on the phone. He was coming back over to give her the sedative she had refused. When he arrived he looked very serious, which was unusual for the good-natured doctor. He made Rachel sit down next to her granddaughter.

"I ran some tests myself to get quicker results. I have a very surprising result for you." He hesitated searching for the right words. "My dear, Mariah, you are pregnant." He took a deep gulp, the women were both silent.

"I ... I knew I was late, but I thought it was just from being so upset since Joe ..." Her voice softly faded out without finishing her thought.

It took Rachel a minute to fully comprehend the unexpected news. She put her arm around Mariah.

"Honey, I know this is a shock, but think about it. This is Joe's and your child. The two of you created this child from the tremendous love you shared. It's a precious part of him that will go on. I know it is overwhelming, but it's wonderful news in this time of sadness, a blessing, truly a blessing."

Chapter 8

The morning of the funeral dawned exceptionally warm for early May, in New England. Mariah sat alone on the sun porch, trying to think about the baby, but mostly thinking about Joe. They had met three years earlier when he had come into her real estate office inquiring about some development property. He was tall and slender with auburn hair and hazel eyes. When he looked at her she felt like he could see into her soul. There was an instant attraction that quickly turned to passionate love. They were married four months after they met. Only six months later Joe was called to active duty and sent to Iraq.

After his first tour of duty, he was allowed to come home on leave for a month. They had spent the first three days locked in their house making passionate love. When they finally emerged there were twenty-three messages on the answering machine, mostly from Mariah's office. She remembered how they had laughed listening to some of the sarcastic comments in the messages. But they did not care what anyone thought, they were completely lost in their own blissful world. It went so quickly, and too soon he was gone back to the war. Shortly after his return, his plane was shot down. It was so hard to believe she would never see him again. She could not imagine life without him.

Rachel came into the sun porch. She wore a deep purple tailored suit, which looked stunning with her silver hair pulled back in a knotted bun. She had simple diamond studs on her ears and her beautiful gold pendant around her neck. Even at seventy years old she could turn heads with her striking beauty.

"Mariah, the Limousine is here." Rachel offered her a hand. "Honey, are you ready?"

"I'll never be ready for this Grand ... but I want to be dignified to honor Joe and make him proud of me." She took Rachel's hand.

"You look lovely. I am so glad you chose not to wear black. This rose colored dress seems very appropriate and looks so nice with your dark hair. The color is very representative of love you know, and your special cross is perfect with it." She straightened the necklace and kissed her granddaughter's cheek. "Joe is very proud of you, sweetie!"

The military funeral seemed to go quickly. Chaplain Santini gave a brief generalized eulogy, since Rachel purposely never returned his calls. A couple of Joe's college friends spoke, and then a cousin, he really didn't have many living relatives. Lastly, John Benson spoke. Although he had known Joe the shortest time, his remembrance was the most touching. He spoke of trust between two people, and how quickly you must learn to trust another pilot you are flying missions with. He told how Joe had shot down a missile, which would have hit his plane. Later when he tried to thank Joe, he just grinned and said, "I've got your back, buddy. Don't ever worry, I've always got your back!"

John was crying now, as he looked compassionately at Mariah. "Joe, now I promise you. I will help your loved ones in any way I can. I've got your back, buddy, and I always will."

She held the folded flag in her lap, as people filed by her and Grand with their condolences. Soon they were all gone, but a few. Dr. James was by Grand's side, watching over Mariah. Peter, the soldier from the airfield had lingered. He came over and took Mariah's hand telling her he would be in touch to see how she was doing. She smiled politely, even though he made her a bit uncomfortable. After all, he may have been Joe's friend but he was still a stranger to her. John Benson offered his condolences still teary-eyed. Rachel felt sorry for this sincere young man. He obviously had been a good friend to Joe. She personally extended an invitation to him to come back to her home after the funeral. Then of course Chaplain Santini offered his condolences once again, but this time only to the widow, while basically ignoring Rachel. This was not lost on Rachel, she thought good, maybe he got the message.

A few close friends were invited back to Grand's house for refreshments afterwards. Rachel had also graciously invited Joe's military escort. John had come with a couple other soldiers. Unfortunately Santini had the nerve to show up, too.

Rachel served James a glass of wine, as her literary agent, Joan talked his ear off about New York society. He was listening politely.

Mariah was in her favorite chair on the sun porch with a group of young women around her. Some worked for her, others were old friends. They were all babbling and gossiping, obviously trying to lighten the moment for Mariah. Every now and then, there would be a burst of laughter or the sound of Ahhs. Rachel smiled to herself thinking how good this was for Mariah, who had become so isolated since Joe's death. It gave her too much time to dwell on her loss. The phone rang, and Rachel hurried towards the study to answer it, so she could hear above the noise of the company. She bumped into the Chaplain coming around the corner, from the direction of her study. He seemed even more nervous than usual.

"Oh, sorry, I was just looking for the bathroom."

Rachel eyed him suspiciously, "The bathroom is at the other end of the house, and now if you will excuse me." The phone was still ringing incessantly.

"Hello, hello …"

There was no one speaking. She said hello one more time, but all she could hear was heavy breathing at the other end of the line. She slammed the phone down right as James came into the room looking for her.

"What's wrong Rachel?" He looked very concerned.

"Oh nothing, just some prank caller that has been bothering me. I hope I hurt his ear!" She laughed.

"Well, there's been quite a bit of publicity over Joe's death, and that tends to bring the nuts out. You might consider getting an unlisted number."

"My gallant James, ever the caretaker! I'll be fine with this number. Are you leaving?"

"Yes, I get the distinct feeling Joan would like some quality time with you," he said looking over the top of his glasses at her. "She's quite a beauty!"

Rachel laughed, hooking her arm in his to walk him to the door. "She is one of a kind! James, thank you for all your help these past weeks. It is so nice to have someone in our lives we know we can trust."

"Come on, Rach, you know you two ladies are like family to me. When Mariah is feeling up to it she needs to come in for a full examine, and I'll refer her to an obstetrician. Do you think she will have this baby?"

"My God, James I hadn't considered anything else! I certainly hope so!"

"Now don't get excited. Young women today do have options. I don't know how she feels, but it does need to be her decision." With that James leaned over and gave Rachel a quick kiss on the lips. He smiled with a familiar twinkle in his eyes, which Rachel had grown to love. "I'll call you."

She closed the door and leaned against it, suddenly feeling exhausted she closed her eyes; it had been a long day. Her brief moment of peace was broken by the raspy voice of her agent.

"Rachel, Hon, I've been dying to speak with you about the manuscript since I got here. How are we doing on it?"

Joan took a slow sip of wine watching Rachel walk over to the wingback chair by the fireplace. Rachel flipped the switch for the gas fireplace, the flickering flames always helped her relax. It was for this reason alone she had the three fireplaces in her big Victorian house converted to gas. She motioned for her agent to sit across from her in the matching chair.

"I have managed to get a few chapters done in all the confusion." Rachel hesitated, watching the comforting flames dance in the fireplace. "I know the legend so well, it is not difficult for me to write it in story form. With Joe's funeral over, life should settle down a bit, although I plan to try my best to get Mariah to move back home permanently."

"Well, it won't interfere with your writing will it? I mean, doesn't your granddaughter have a real estate business to run?" Joan asked rather anxiously.

Rachel smiled, "of course, Joan. We all know time is money." Rachel liked egging her on with her own kind of thinking. "Let me get the copy I printed for you. Maybe you can read it on the flight back to the city, then call me tomorrow with your thoughts on it?"

"Fabulous, darling, fabulous!" Joan exclaimed, as both women rose from their chairs.

Chapter 9

Mariah stayed at her grandmother's house for two weeks following the funeral. It was actually, what she needed, for a short time anyway. Grand pampered her, shielding her from the outside world. All phone calls were screened through the answering machine. It was apparent to Rachel that the same crackpot was calling her granddaughter repeatedly, saying some bizarre things about loving her. Yet, she felt it would be unnecessarily upsetting to tell Mariah about these calls, assuming he would eventually give up.

Rachel was rising at dawn each day and writing fervently, in her study for hours. Mariah was starting to sleep a little better; she wasn't waking up until mid-morning most days. Often the two of them would take late morning walks on the beach. Then Rachel would make her a scrumptious brunch, but what she appreciated most was her grandmother's unwavering patience. She listened to Mariah talk about Joe and what happened to him over and over again. It was a necessary process, attempting to understand Joe's tragedy, piecing it together, and somehow fitting it into her reality. Yet, she would have felt uncomfortable talking in such length about his death with anyone else.

Grand had even accompanied her to Joe's grave the first time she went back because she feared going. The nightmares were different now. She was usually running or hiding from someone in the cemetery, sensing an evil presence, but never really seeing anyone. Yet, what really disturbed her in these dreams was the feeling that Joe was warning her of some kind of danger. She tried to dismiss the nightmares as a combination of grief and changing hormones, but they still terrified her.

Grand had also shared more of the family legend with her. Although Mariah wondered if it was actually a story about their ancestors, she was fascinated with the legend. She found she could identify with Mary, the young widow in the story. And knowing her grandmother she figured this was no coincidence.

Mariah's coworkers at the real estate office were calling and coming to see her about business more each day. She was considering going back to the office soon. The sale of summer homes was booming, and her three-girl office could barely handle the number of clientele wanting to buy and sell waterfront property.

She started Coastal Sandcastles right after she had graduated from college. The business quickly became the premier real estate company for high-end waterfront properties, in the exclusive coastal town where she lived. The real estate market was extremely lucrative right now, but she knew it could vacillate without warning. She had been thinking a lot about how expensive it would be raising a child as a single mother. She had made some important decisions, although she had not shared them with anyone yet. The first was more of a realization that she already loved the baby she was carrying. Her second decision was that she would raise this child the way she and Joe would have together. And the third was, her child would be loved more than anyone else in the world. She planned to provide the best of everything for this child, just as if there were two parents. Consequently, she needed to get back to work and keep her business booming for as long as possible.

Sitting in the sun porch, sipping ice tea, she announced to Grand she would be going back to her condo the next day and to work the following Monday.

Rachel began to object, but then thought better of it. Instead, she offered support, saying she would help in any way possible. She saw a glimmer of the strong young woman Mariah used to be and felt she should encourage her.

"Grand, I also want you to know I have a doctor's appointment next week, and I will be scheduling them regularly for the next seven months." She smiled at her grandmother, knowing how she felt about this baby.

"Oh, sweetie, I am so happy for you, for us, for the baby!" She hugged her granddaughter for a long time. "We will have much to prepare to welcome this little baby. And please, Mariah, will you think about coming back here to live? There is plenty of room for both of you in this big old rambling house. Besides, I could be a really convenient babysitter." She winked, they both laughed, and Mariah agreed to think about it.

Rachel left the room to answer the phone. Mariah could hear her raise her voice a bit and guessed it was Joan Hale. The pushy agent had been calling three and four times a day, harassing Rachel to get the book done. She returned to the room quite flustered.

"If I didn't want this story known so much I would fire this woman right now! She wants me to send her every word, as soon as it is written! Ridiculous! I should have never given her those first couple of chapters. I told her she will get what I have when I am ready to send it to her!" Rachel sank into the cushioned chair exasperated.

"Grand, you will probably be able to get more done with me out from underfoot."

"Nonsense, I have been writing steadily everyday. This insane agent simply wants the book done yesterday." Rachel sighed, gazing at the calm sea outside.

"And don't forget Mariah, I want you to know the whole story before anyone else." She rubbed the pendant between her forefinger and thumb, as her thoughts drifted to the true story of her ancestors.

"Grand, what if you email each chapter to me before you send it to Joan? That way I could read it first, and have a copy for myself before it's even published."

"Excellent idea, my dear, excellent! I will be sending you two very important chapters in the next day or so. Then we will talk about the legend. Now let's get you packed." Rising from her chair Rachel took Mariah's hand affectionately and led the way.

Chapter 10

It seemed like dawn would never come to the young woman who nervously sat at the edge of her bed. Tossing and turning she had not been able to sleep much during the night. She had slept so much the night before, she could not settle down.

Finally, the blackened night sky started to fade to gray with the onset of daylight. Mary was impatient and wanted to be ready to go to her husband's grave when the sun rose on the horizon. She quickly went about washing her face and brushing her long hair until each strand was in just the right place.

From her wardrobe she chose a crimson silk gown with some delicate embroidery at the neckline. As the dress fell down over her slender body, the rich fabric felt cool against her skin. Next, she tied a long cord of golden silk around her waist that when knotted hung to the hemline of her dress and defined her small waist.

On her feet she wore beautiful sandals that had the same embroidery design as her dress. Scandalous she knew, but she just could not wear the dreary robes of widowhood. He had always loved how she looked in her colorful dresses.

"You are beautiful," he would say as she regally danced before him, twisting and turning in alluring poses. She was wearing it for him. She would be beautiful for him.

Suddenly, while dressing, a wave of dizziness came over Mary causing her to sit down on the bed. Her stomach was queasy. She had not eaten much the day before. Even dinner had not appealed to Mary, and Ruth had made a fuss about keeping up her strength. She sat for a few minutes and the symptoms seemed to pass, leaving only her stomach still feeling uneasy.

Mary slowly got up, quietly opening her bedroom door. The last thing she wanted to do was to awaken her brother and sister. She needed this time alone at her husband's grave to acknowledge his passing and learn to live with the separation. Would they really see each other in the next life? He would talk to her about his beliefs, and now she so wanted his teachings to be true. She could not imagine an eternity without him.

Passing the kitchen table on her way to the door, Mary picked up some fruited bread left from the night before.

She needed to quiet her empty stomach. Outside her home the world about her was quiet. She breathed deeply of the cool morning air. The sun was just peaking over the horizon.

Quickly passing through the gardens, with a distance to go, she hurried. She wanted to be alone and did not want to meet anyone along the way.

Mary new the way to Joseph's estate, but the short trip seemed to take much longer than she originally thought. The houses she passed were still quiet with sleep. She knew the people who occupied them and was grateful their day had not yet begun. Except for her years at the temple, she had lived amongst them, but now she did not want to speak to anyone, nor see the pity in their eyes. She needed the peace and quiet of the early morning to herself, even if it was selfish of her.

Her footsteps quickened when she saw the beautiful gardens in the distance ahead. Coming closer she could smell the sweetness of the fruit trees and blossoming flowers. The many trees offered shelter from the scorching sun. It was such an oasis in this desert land they lived in. Mary was grateful to her husband's friend for offering this burial place. Thanks to Joseph's generosity, her husband had a beautiful resting place she would be able to visit often.

She sheltered her eyes from the bright sun. It was going to be a hot day. She squinted as she searched for the rock formation that was her husband's burial place.

Everything had happened so quickly on the day he died, she had not paid attention to the exact location. She had been too distraught to make any decisions, so had left them to the men. She needed to look for the large boulder, which had been rolled across the entrance to the grave.

Mary's heart began to pound, her pulse quickening when she spotted the burial site. She was anxious and scared at the same time. She had so much she wanted to say to him, yet she wanted to run in the opposite direction. For a moment, she wished she had someone with her for support, but she was alone.

She slowed her pace, as she circled the rocks marking her husband's grave. Suddenly she froze. "I can't do this. Oh, God, give me strength," she cried in desperation as a tear trickled down her flushed cheek. Fear engulfed her. Finally, her prayer was answered, and she found the strength to move toward the tomb. She was horrified at what she saw and screamed.

"Oh, God, No!" her voice cried as she drew nearer the spot. Her knees gave out from under her, and she sank to the dusty earth, her head in her hands. A flood of tears streamed from her eyes and her whole body trembled.

The large boulder had been moved to one side of the grave. The tomb, which had only days before held the dead body of her husband, now lay empty. Sunlight filled the opening, there could be no mistake, his body was gone.

The young widow was a sorrowful sight. Her voice trembled as she softly called her husband's name. Her heart was calling him from the depths of her pain as if to say, "Where are you?" Her arms folded across her knees, she rocked back and forth, repeating her husband's name. The mantra continued for a long time.

She was alone with no one to cradle and comfort her. No one heard her sorrowful wailing voice. Her cries and the rocking motion of her body had propelled her into another world. It wouldn't have mattered if someone were by her side, she was alone with her pain.

Deep within her sorrow, she could gently, faintly hear a voice calling her name. "Mary, my beloved." She was startled, but recognized the voice of her husband. She raised her tear-stained face looking frantically in each direction. Her spirits were lifted, as the voice continued to call her a smile came to her lips.

Suddenly he was in front of her, lifting her up and pulling her into his arms. He soothed her with his warm voice as his hands tenderly stroked her hair and face. He held her tightly. Once more she was gently wrapped in his loving arms and felt whole again. Her sobs slowly subsided, and time stood still for these two lovers. His presence gave Mary strength. Her wet eyes became dry with wonder as she adoringly gazed upon her husband. She had much to say to him, but her words lay locked inside her. Their hearts silently spoke a lifetime of love. Gone were the pain and tears, and her heart was no longer broken.

Mary had seen her beloved and knew of his undying love for her. In her heart she knew his love would always be with her, guiding her. She was filled with peace.

"Mary," he whispered her name again. "Mary, I must be going. Go, tell the others you have seen me," he commanded gently.

"Remember, I am with you always. Be peaceful in this knowledge. Go." He quickly disappeared from her sight.

For a few minutes, Mary stood gazing into the distance, smiling. He was gone, but his love had replaced the ache in her heart.

His words echoed in the silence, "Go, tell the others you have seen me." Finally, she forced herself to move, now anxious to tell the others of this wondrous moment. Mary felt empowered to do as her husband had asked. The garden was no longer a fearful place. This day had brought great joy, and she would hold it in her heart forever.

Chapter 11

The garden was still quiet, but the chirping of a nearby bird brought Mary back to reality. Knowing her family would be worried about her, Mary slowly left the burial place and headed towards home. She would share the news with her sister and brother before going into town to tell the others.

When earlier she doubted her ability to live without her husband, Mary now knew she had the courage to go on. She knew life would not be easy, but she would survive.

Unlike most new widows, Mary did not have to worry about food and shelter. With money from the family vineyards, she was a wealthy independent woman capable of caring for herself. She would continue to live on the family estate.

Mary's worry had been about the emptiness in her heart. In the time she and her husband had been together they had shared a great deal. They had much in common and could talk for hours on many subjects.

They first met on a hillside in Galilee where he had been preaching to a small group of people. She was passing along the roadside from Northern Galilee enroute to her family estate in the South. Her traveling party stopped to watch the young man for a few minutes.

By the way he carried himself, she could see he was confident in his teaching abilities and had the attention of those around him. Wanting to hear him speak, she went closer, standing on the outside of the circle. Warmth and caring came forth in his words. He was gifted she thought.

When he was done speaking he left the circle and headed in her direction. He had seen her arrive and had wondered what an Egyptian priestess was doing in his midst.

"My lady," he greeted her warmly. "Have you come to learn more about my heavenly father?" he teasingly asked.

"No," she quickly replied with a smile on her lips. "The goddess Isis reigns in the heavens and bestows her blessings on her devoted subjects. Of that I am confident. I am her humble priestess.

"Yes, I could see that by the emblem on your cloak," he replied. "I have spent much time in Egypt as a child and of late, so I know well the one you serve."

"Are you preaching in this area too?" he continued.

"Not at the moment," she replied. "I have just come from the temple in the North where I performed a welcoming ceremony for new believers. Now I am going to spend some time with my family before returning to the temple in Alexandria.

They continued to talk for a few more minutes and then said goodbye. He returned to his group, and she continued her travels.

One day, during her visit home, her brother came into the house announcing he had invited a friend to dinner. When the friend arrived, Mary was surprised to see the preacher she had met on the road a few days earlier.

When introductions were made, Mary's brother was surprised to learn his sister had previously met his friend.

"She came to hear me preach on the kingdom of God," he teased.

"I would be foolish not to stop and listen. After all, I must know my competition," she returned spiritedly.

There was lively conversation in the household that evening along with much laughter. The two preachers were equals and enjoyed challenging the other's thoughts and comments. Both were passionate in their beliefs, she in the service of the ancient goddess, and he to his god. Her brother's friend returned a number of times during the remainder of Mary's visit. A friendship was growing between the two, and Mary's brother was pleased. At the end of her stay, Mary said she would soon visit her family again.

Temple celebrations kept Mary in Alexandria longer than she had first anticipated. There were high holy days to be celebrated and ceremonies of initiation to preside over. Besides her teaching in the temple, there were always the anointing of the dead and fertility rites to perform. She went about her tasks joyfully encouraging others to do the same.

When she was able, Mary again set out for Galilee. She loved the role of itinerant preacher best. She met wonderful people along the way and could see for herself the people adored the goddess. As the earthly representative of the goddess, Mary was also loved, and it was always her privilege to serve the people of Isis.

When in Galilee, if time allowed, Mary would seek the whereabouts of the preacher to greet him. When she was free she would accompany him as he traveled the countryside preaching and ministering to ever-growing crowds. She noticed how curious people were about the young Rabbi. His words were powerful and fascinating to those who stayed to listen, making a difference in their lives. She enjoyed his positive message, and over a period of months she found herself becoming a devoted listener. Their conversations turned to teaching sessions for Mary. She was able to question and challenge some of his ideas. He never rebuked her thoughts or ideas and was always open to what she had to say, praising her for the courage to speak her mind. He had told her many times he wished others could understand his teachings with the depth that she did.

They soon became constant companions, and some of his friends were jealous of their loving relationship and her intellectual ability. But, he had a way of appeasing them, thereby making Mary feel comfortable. She would miss those wonderful times spent together.

Mary's feet quickened as she neared her home. She could see Ruth was waiting for her at the front door.

"Mary," called Ruth as she left the doorway and ran down the dirt road to meet her sister. The two embraced.

"We have been worried about you. You left so early."

"I needed to be alone with my thoughts. I am well and have much to tell you," said Mary excitedly as the two walked towards their home.

"I saw him!" Mary exclaimed to her sister.

Ruth saw the sparkle in her sister's eyes and marveled at the change that had come over her since the evening before. She had been inconsolable, now she was vibrant and alive.

"Come, let me tell you," Mary said as she led her sister into the house, with words already flowing from her.

Ruth listened attentively, and soon she was as excited as her sister about the events of the past couple hours.

"I must go tell the others," emphasized Mary as she concluded her story.

"First you must eat. I will prepare something while you wash up and change your clothes," Ruth insisted. "You cannot go out looking like that," she continued pointing to Mary's wrinkled dress. Ruth sounded like a mother admonishing her child.

Once in her room she realized how dirty she had become. Her face was streaked with dusty tears, and her once beautiful dress was wrinkled as though it has been pulled from a heap.

"Ruth's right." she declared as she poured water from the pitcher in her room.

It was mid morning with the sun already high in the sky, but Mary's body felt as though it was midnight. She was emotionally exhausted from the last twenty-four hours and longed to lie down and nap.

As Mary lay back on the bed, she thought she would rest for a few minutes while Ruth prepared the food. Her body quickly relaxed and soon her eyes began to close. Sleep was such a powerful opiate she could not fight it.

"Mary, Mary," a gentle voice called.

Startled she opened her eyes, wondering if she had been dreaming. Again she heard a voice calling her. This time she recognized Ruth's voice at her door.

"Come, your food is ready," Ruth, whispered through the opened door.

Mary quickly sat up, rubbing the sleep from her eyes. How long had she slept? It couldn't have been very long because she didn't feel rested. She must have dozed off for only a moment, yet she had a strange dream.

Hurriedly she threw on a cool lightweight robe and slipped her feet into more comfortable sandals for walking. Within moments she was by her sister's side in the kitchen, gratefully taking a bowl of food from Ruth's hand.

She was hungry, but the food was too hot to eat. Mary mindlessly stirred the meal in front of her, as her thoughts drifted back to her dream.

"Aren't you hungry?" Ruth asked as she watched her sister.

"I am, but I was just thinking about a dream I had."

"A dream?"

"It's the only way I can explain it. It all happened so fast, yet seemed so real. Just before you called me, I laid down on my bed to rest and drifted off to sleep. I heard someone calling my name, and suddenly there was an angel standing beside my bed, telling me I am with child. Then I heard you calling me and realized I must have been dreaming. It was very strange, yet very real."

"Maybe that was god's way of telling you that you are going to have a baby." Ruth looked at her questioningly.

"With all that has happened I never considered that possibility," said Mary.

"You certainly haven't paid much attention to the signs you have been experiencing. Besides, with the death of your husband, that would be the last thing on your mind. If this is true, Mary, what a joy!" she said with excitement in her voice. "It would be wonderful to have a little one in this house. Imagine, having his child to love and raise."

Ruth was right, it would be wonderful she thought.

Was she really carrying his child? She certainly could be, but she had not given much thought to the idea until now. Dare she hope for this to be true? All these thoughts and more went through her mind as she quietly placed her hand on her belly, and a single tear of joy escaped from her eye. This was a bittersweet moment in her life.

"I cannot dwell on this dream anymore," said Mary. "I must go and tell the others what I saw. I'm not sure where they are all staying, but I will find them. Don't worry about me, I promise to be back by sunset."

"May God bless you," said Ruth as she watched her sister set out on her journey.

It was a long walk in the scorching sun. It was not yet the noon hour, but already the cool morning air was gone. The young widow walked on with determination and excitement arriving at Timothy's house first. No one was at home, so she proceeded into town in search of Peter and the others. She stopped at Andrew's home, and he opened the door and greeted her warmly. He gently kissed her on the cheek as she entered.

As she crossed the threshold, she saw the room was filled with many of her husband's friends. Each in turn greeted her as Andrew had done. She felt welcome.

"I have wonderful news," exclaimed Mary as she freely began to speak. "I was at the tomb just after sunrise this morning, and I saw him. After talking to him, he asked me to come and tell you."

Suddenly there was silence in the room. Peter stepped forward, showing concern for his friend's widow. "Mary, are you sure of what you have seen? I know how distraught you were when we buried him," looking at her sympathetically.

"I know what I saw," she insisted. "It was not a vision. I did see my husband. I talked with him, and he consoled me. The last thing he asked of me was to come and tell this to you. I have done as he asked, yet you don't believe me." She was sadly disappointed with their disbelief.

Murmurings could be heard across the room. "Let's go to the tomb and see for ourselves." They all agreed.

Peter led the men hurriedly from the room, leaving Mary alone. Silently she left Andrew's house feeling hurt and disappointed. She had expected jubilation over her husband's words, but she had not been believed. Saddened, she turned and headed in the direction of her home. Knowing she would be home earlier than she had first told her sister.

Chapter 12

Rachel reread the two recent chapters one more time, and then hit send. She was a little apprehensive about telling Mariah such important family history in this manner. Yet, with how busy she was with her real estate business, and the pressure Rachel was feeling from her agent, it was the best way to assure Mariah would know everything before publication.

Mariah hung up the phone, it was another one of those calls. Whoever was calling would just stay on the line breathing heavy, the calls came so often that Amy had named the person the silent caller. Shrugging off the calls as nothing more than a prank, she leaned back in her chair, and stretched her legs. It had been about a month since she had come back to the office, and it felt good to be working, concentrating on something other than her loss. She was still having some very sad days when she missed Joe tremendously, but found if she occupied her time with work she wouldn't dwell on it. Her clothes had started getting tight in the waist, and when she looked in the mirror she could see a potbelly starting to show. She was over her morning sickness now, but still having a difficult time imagining having a baby, especially without her husband.

The bell on the office door rang, announcing someone had entered. Mariah looked up to see a very handsome man dressed immaculately in a short-sleeved navy blue shirt, khaki pants, and boating shoes without socks. He looked like he had just stepped off one of the yachts docked down the street from her office. It took her a minute to realize who he was. John Benson stood there grinning at her.

Good morning, Mariah"

"Why good morning, John," Mariah replied unable to hide her surprise at seeing him.

John stammered a little with an explanation as he told her he was now a civilian. After serving twelve years in the service Iraq had done him in. He could not tolerate witnessing, or being part of any more bloodshed. Joe's death had been the final straw for him.

"I wanted to see how you are doing and also if you can help me find a place to live." Now he looked at her questioningly.

She had not noticed in earlier meetings how handsome he was. His deep blue eyes were mesmerizing. They caught Mariah by surprise, and now it was she who stumbled over her words. She could feel her face flush, so she turned to her desk pretending to look at some listings, giving her time to regain her composure.

"Please have a seat, John. Let's see what you are looking for, and I'll see if I know of a match." She looked up smiling.

John looked at her kindly. "Okay, but first tell me how you are doing?"

"Honestly John, I take it one day at a time. Some days are much worse than others."

Mariah twisted her wedding band. "I miss him terribly." She hesitated then looked up. "I've had a lot of unexpected anger to deal with too. Coming back to work has helped take my mind off of his death for part of the day, but even then well-meaning people say things that are so upsetting to me. Things like God doesn't give you more than you can handle, or God works in mysterious ways, or my favorite, there is a reason he died young."

A tear rolled down Mariah's cheek. "I'm sorry, John. I don't mean to unload on you. I just get so angry. God didn't do this. Man did it! There is no justification for Joe's death, and there never will be."

"It's all right, Mariah," John said softly. "I agree with you. My reasons for returning to civilian life, when I was intending to be a lifer, are for similar reasons." He reached across the desk gently patting her hand.

Just then the bell on the door rang as someone entered. Mariah quickly pulled her hand away from John's, but not before Helen, the biggest gossip in town, viewed the scene.

"Oh, excuse me. I hope I am not interrupting?" She looked from Mariah to John, and back again, waiting for an answer.

"Not at all, Helen, can I help you?" Mariah walked briskly around the desk intentionally blocking her view of John. Helen smiled, going to the free magazines, saying she just stopped to pick up the latest real estate books for a friend. When she lingered, as though wanting to meet John, Mariah walked towards the door and said curtly, "Sure, take one of each, and do have your friend call me." She didn't believe for a moment there was a friend because she knew from past experience how nosy Helen was.

Sure enough, Helen turned as she was leaving and said, "Oh, congratulations on your expected bundle of joy."

Mariah simply smiled holding the door open for her. She turned back to John after putting the closed sign up.

"Sorry, it is a small town, and since Joe's death everybody thinks my life is their business. Now tell me what you are looking for and what kind of budget we have to work with."

"Okay ... but did I hear right? Well, it's not my business, but ..."

"It's alright, John. It's not a secret that I am pregnant. Actually, I only found out after I fainted at the airfield that day. My due date is at the end of December, so it must have happened just before Joe left for his second tour."

"I think it's wonderful, Mariah. Joe would have been very proud."

An hour later she locked the door behind him, as he waved. They had made a list of possible homes for him. He left armed with the addresses to drive by before setting up any appointments. She was glad he wanted to do that since it usually saved her time.

She sat back down thinking about what a nice man he seemed to be and understood why Joe would have befriended him. Turning to the computer, she checked her email one more time before calling it a day. It was only three o'clock, but she was very tired. Quickly surveying her email, she opened one from Grand. Mariah was excited to see it was more of the family legend and started to read it, but then decided to print it out to read at home.

Chapter 13

Rachel was engrossed in writing the next chapter of her book when the phone rang. She ignored it, letting the machine get it, but when she heard Mariah's voice she grabbed the phone.

"Hello dear, how are you?"

"Hi Grand, I'm good. I just finished reading your latest chapters, and I have some questions."

"Yes, I thought you might."

"Some of this sounds so familiar to me. Have I heard this story before?"

"Yes, you have heard parts of the story before, but never all of it," she sighed. "Why don't you come over for dinner? I'll explain more then."

"That sounds great. I am going to take a short nap right now, so is an hour good? And can I bring anything?"

"An hour is fine, don't rush. Just bring yourself and of course that little baby." Rachel grinned. She was so excited about her great-grandchild she had already started picking up little baby things.

Mariah yawned as she hung the phone up. She leaned her head back in her chair quickly falling asleep. Once again, she was in the cemetery, she was running, looking over her shoulder. There was a dark figure lurking behind a tree, then behind a large headstone. It was getting closer. Breathing heavily now, she was attempting to reach her car, just ahead. She could feel Joe urging her to go faster. Quickly locking the doors she fumbled trying to start the car just as a heavy hand came down on her right shoulder. She awoke with a start, soaked with perspiration. Jumping out of her chair she looked behind her. Rubbing her shoulder she could still feel the weight of something sinister on it.

On the drive to Grand's house Mariah still had chills thinking about her nightmare. *I'll certainly be glad when these hormones straighten out. I'm losing it when I actually start checking the back seat before I get in the car.* She told herself. Even so, the lights of her grandmother's house were a comforting sight.

It was a pleasant June evening, and dinner was served on the sun porch with all the windows open. A soft sea breeze wafted through the room causing the flames on the candles to cast dancing shadows around the room. After the table was cleared they moved to the cozy wicker chairs to have their tea. They sat quietly for a time, both satisfied to simply listen to the gentle sound of waves breaking on the nearby beach. Mariah was so relaxed and content she was lost in thought staring at one of the candles.

"So my dear, you find the story I have written so far familiar?" Rachel studied her granddaughter, curious about what her reaction would be as she came to understand the importance of the legend being revealed to her. And even more importantly, how would she feel about her connection to this incredible truth?

"Yes Grand, it sounds like something I learned when I was young."

"Well that's because you have heard similar versions in your religious education classes, but you have never heard the complete and true story. Very few have." Rachel seemed to turn quite serious, as she fingered her pendant. "The story goes back thousands of years. The truth has always been suppressed out of fear of feminine power."

"I don't understand, Grand. Suppressed by whom?" She sipped her tea looking perplexed.

"Suppressed by men, Mariah. Please bare with me, dear. None of this will be easy to understand, much less accept."

Now Rachel sipped her tea as she thought about where to start. "I know you studied Women's History while you were at Smith College. Do you remember the Women's Holocaust? Or the period from the 11th to the 18th century often referred to as The Burning Times? It was a time when thousands of women were senselessly killed in Europe."

"I do remember some about it, but I didn't study it in depth."

"Let me refresh your memory. It was the worse in Germany. In one town they ran out of seasoned wood to heat with for the winter because they burned so many women to death. Another town had only one woman left in it when they were finished their witch hunt. They had women turning on each other out of fear; mothers turning on daughters, sisters turning on sisters, neighbors on neighbors. They accused each other of being evil, of being witches, in an attempt to save themselves." Rachel sighed and took a sip of her tea. "It's estimated anywhere from 30,000 to 100,000 women were burned to death in one year in Germany."

"The tortures they endured were horrific. I am sure you have heard of the saying, 'The Third Degree.' The term is actually derived from the last torture performed on these women attempting to force them to confess to witchcraft. If they didn't confess, they died being tortured. And if they did, they were burned at the stake. This massive witch-hunt was all a fabrication of the church.

It began as a quest for control over the people, but became so profitable it turned into a quest for riches. You see land was wealth back then, and wealth was power. The men of the church discovered it was simple to acquire the properties of women and others by accusing them of evil doings, thus assuring they were powerless. Anyone who did not follow church doctrine strictly was considered a heretic and ordered put to death. The wealthier the men became, the more powerful and greedier they became, so the killing continued for centuries."

"I do remember learning some of this at Smith, Grand, but I don't understand what this has to do with your book or our family legend."

"Patience my dear, you will understand in time."

Rachel stood and stretched, then poured them each a fresh cup of tea.

"It's interesting with all the efforts to restrain feminine power down through the ages women have never been totally suppressed. And we never can be because no one can take away our spirituality. We are the backbones of our families. We are the essence of spirituality and always have been. Certainly you remember learning about the Salem witch trials?" Mariah nodded yes.

"Well, that was a carry over from what happened in Europe. It was absolutely a continuation of the attempt by men to brand women as evil to assure they would remain powerless."

"I never quite thought of it in that light Grand, but it makes sense."

"Mariah, the oppression of women worldwide to this day stems back through history to our ancestral story; which all men of faith have chosen to discredit or deny for the last two thousand years. Are you beginning to understand?"

"I am not sure Grand, what I'm thinking would be incredible if true. I mean the idea of our ancestors ... I can't be thinking the right thing ... Who, Who exactly was Mary's husband?"

Chapter 14

"Mariah, listen to me. I am writing this book and revealing our story because it is time the world knows the truth. The time has come for women to take their rightful places in society and within the church."

"But Grand ..."

"No, wait let me finish. For the last fifty or so years there has been a quiet women's movement going on behind the radical feminist movement, which has received so much negative attention. Think about the large numbers of older women who are going back to school. And the massive numbers of young women who have been quietly working their way into powerful positions in government, education, finance, and science. The positions they have attained are not by accident. Consider women like Senator Hillary Clinton, or Gloria Steinem. Or Oprah Winfrey, the greatest humanitarian of our times, and even Mother Theresa, who was a living saint. These are only a few of the strong women who have had worldwide influence through positions they attained. Globally they have helped the advancement of women tremendously.

Meanwhile, many men are arrogantly depending more and more on their gender to gain positions of power. And sadly less and less young men are even going to college." Rachel took another sip of tea and paused to catch her breath. She was thrilled to finally be sharing all of this with her granddaughter.

"The Vatican has repeatedly denounced feminists as wanting to overpower men, which we all know is simply untrue. Women only want to be recognized and acknowledged as the equals they are and always have been. This Mariah is why now is the time for our family legend to be told to the world! The danger in telling it has diminished more and more with the increasing arrogance of men.

Look at men's abuse of power worldwide in many different areas: we see it by CEOs in business, by priests in churches, and by top officials in government."

"Grand, I still do not see the connection between all of this and our ancestral story. Who were our ancestors? And why would their story have such an impact on history?"

"I think you have already guessed the incredible answer to your first question. Mary's husband was Jesus."

Although Mariah had suspected the answer to her question, she sat dumbfounded for a few minutes. Rachel waited silently, as her granddaughter contemplated this incredible information.

"Are you serious Grand—Jesus was married? And Mary Magdalene ... They were our ancestors?" Mariah walked to the window and turned back to Rachel, half expecting her to say she was kidding. But she could read the expression on her grandmother's face and knew she was quite serious.

"I know it sounds unbelievable. I reacted the same way when my grandmother told me, and your mother reacted the same way when she was told. Yet, it is true. It is very important that you have faith and believe Mariah because we are the last of the bloodline." Rachel was holding her hand to her chest covering the gold pendant she always wore close to her heart.

"Do you understand how the denial of their relationship and long ago story has contributed to the oppression of women down through time?"

"I think I see Grand, but this is too much for me to absorb all at once. I need to think all of this through." She sat down again and stared at the candle.

"Sweetie, I know this is all pretty shocking. But as you read the full story in my manuscript, you will come to understand how finally telling the true story of Jesus and Mary will help restore the equality we were robbed of so long ago. Most men will denounce this story, but the majority of women will embrace it. That will be a step towards finally taking our rightful place alongside of men, instead of following them. Rachel stood now and yawned.

"It is late, and I am tired, you must be also. Stay over, your bed has fresh sheets, and we can chat in the morning." She blew out the candles.

Mariah agreed. "I don't know if I'll sleep thinking about all you have told me, Grand."

"Well, then think about your little baby." She patted Mariah's tummy gently. "Wait until I show you the cute things I bought her."

"Her? It's too soon to know if it's a girl or a boy."

"Oh yes, well I just assumed because of our family history. The firstborn female always seems to have a female, but who knows it could be different this time." They linked arms and walked upstairs together.

Chapter 15

Joan Hale poured over the chapters Rachel had just emailed her. She thought she had read them wrong, but she hadn't. Rachel was definitely alluding to biblical characters, yet she had told Joan this was a true story of her ancestry. If this story were for real thought the agent it would be worth a fortune. Pressing the intercom button she asked her assistant to get Cardinal Thomas Leary on the line. She had helped him publish two books and considered him an authority on the history of Christianity.

After explaining Rachel's manuscript to him she asked if there could be any truth to this legend.

The Cardinal told her there had always been murmurings that Jesus had been married. Some people claim he was married to Mary Magdalene, and he even considered her his equal. He had heard numerous absurd stories of her having her own ministry and actually being able to perform miracles, as the apostles did after Christ died. Supposedly she wore a gold pendant symbolizing the union of the sacred feminine with the divine masculine. It is said Jesus gave this to her on their wedding day to show that together, as one, they formed the Holy Vessel. Scholars will tell you they have all kinds of proof this story is true, yet the church has always disproved all evidence that has been presented. The church acknowledges she existed. But she was a prostitute Christ saved from being stoned to death and nothing more.

"Very interesting, Thomas," she said quietly.

"I suggest you publish this book as fiction to spare yourself any embarrassment."

"Thank you for your help, Cardinal, I really appreciate it" she replied, blatantly ignoring his suggestion.

"Not at all, Joan, it is always a pleasure to talk with you." He hesitated. "I would be interested in reading this manuscript when it is completed."

"Now, Thomas I couldn't do that. I would be betraying my client's trust, but I would be happy to send you a copy from the first printing."

"Thank you, have a good day, and God bless you, Joan."

Cardinal Leary switched to a secure line, and he was immediately on the phone to the Vatican.

She leaned back in her chair thinking about what the Cardinal had told her. He particularly got her attention when he mentioned the gold pendant. She had immediately thought of Rachel's gold pendant. Ironically, Joan had already asked her about the pendant because she wore it all the time. Rachel had told her it was a cherished family heirloom her grandmother gave her. Sitting contemplating the information Thomas had provided, she had no clue of the wheels that had been set in motion. She could not have imagined the possible danger she had created for Rachel and Mariah.

Chapter 16

John watched Mariah as she drove them to the next house on their list. He hadn't cared for the last two houses, although they had appeared interesting on the outside. The house she was taking him to had just come on the market, and she was raving about it.

He was thinking how beautiful she looked. She had a timeless kind of classic beauty, and he never tired of watching her.

"John, did you hear what I said?"

"Oh, I am sorry. I was just thinking about the view from the last house," he lied.

"I said this house is more expensive than the others because of its location, it is on a bluff overlooking the ocean. I really want you to see it before I tell you the price. Okay?" She gave him a quick smile.

"That's fine, as long as you don't think it's overpriced." He grinned knowing it was her listing.

She turned into a gated drive. The gates were open, but the house was not visible. The driveway was beautifully landscaped on both sides, and as it curved to the right a stately looking colonial came into view on their left. They pulled right up in front.

"What do you think so far?"

"I can see why you love this place. Come on, show me more." He was already out of the car.

They didn't notice they had been followed. A car had parked half way up the driveway, and its occupant had continued on foot, so as not to be detected. Peter peered through some shrubs, spying on them. He had been watching Mariah since the funeral. His previous psychotic behavior had earned him a medical discharge from the service. Unfortunately, long before Joe's funeral he had become obsessed with Mariah. In his own twisted mind he envisioned taking Joe's place in her life and planned to care for Mariah and her baby. He remembered everything Joe had ever said about his wife. That was how he had known to send her yellow roses. Peter had called her grandmother's house repeatedly when she was staying there, hoping to hear her voice, but the old lady always answered. He had really grown to resent her interference, and now John was getting in the way.

Mariah and John entered the house through massive double front doors. The first impression was so stunning they silently stood in the foyer for a long time. On the floor, directly in front of them there was a huge nautical pattern made of inlaid cherry, walnut, and maple, which was striking against the lighter oak floor. Overhead hung an equally impressive large brass onion lamp suspended on a chain from the third floor ceiling. On their right was a grand curved staircase that also appeared to be made of a combination of cherry and walnut with oak treads, partially covered by an exquisite oriental runner. Mariah moved first.

"Come on. There is more to the house than the foyer." They both laughed.

They walked straight ahead into a spacious living room with a view so breathtaking they didn't speak, both walked directly to the wall of glass. All they could see in every direction was the gleaming ocean. There was a large stone patio outside the glass doors, so they stepped outside. It just kept getting more beautiful. The patio was surrounded by fragrant flowering shrubs, with a walkway that led to a pool and Jacuzzi. John stood on the patio trying to absorb the spectacular vista, without even looking at Mariah he asked, "How much?"

"But John, don't you want to see the rest of the property?" He just looked at her. "Okay, it's almost three million." She cringed because it was about a million more than he said he wanted to spend.

"I'll take it! Now show me the rest of my home. We need to get the papers drawn up before anyone else makes an offer." He smiled at her shocked expression.

She was momentarily at a loss for words. "A ... you look around. I'll get the forms out of my car." She was wondering to herself on the way out to the car how he could afford this estate. But that wasn't really her business, as long as he actually could afford it. When she opened the driver side door to get her briefcase she noticed an envelope on the seat, her name was on it. Who would have known where she was? Suddenly she got a chill, feeling as though whoever had put the envelope there was watching her. She locked the car, hurried back into the house and frantically called John three times. He appeared at the upstairs railing, looking down into the foyer.

"Mariah what is it? Are you okay?" He started down the stairs very concerned.

"Yes, it's just strange. I found this envelope on the seat of my car, and I felt like someone was watching me." She waved the envelope nervously in the air for him to see.

"What? Who?" He was coming down the stairs more quickly now. He took her arm. "Come, sit down for a minute." He examined the envelope. "Do you want to open this now?"

"Yes, I want to know who this is and what they want. John, no one knew we were coming here. It's my listing, and it was an afterthought to even bring you here." She paused momentarily, thinking about it. "My God, someone must have been following us!"

Chapter 17

Santini sat with his hand still on the receiver of the phone he had just hung up. He could not believe the Council was entrusting him with such an important request. He could hardly believe they had even contacted him. Thinking about the call he turned his desk fan on. How fortunate that he was a fan of Cardinal Thomas Leary's books. Meeting the Cardinal at his book signings and rubbing elbows with him at various lectures was now going to pay off. Leaning back in his chair he arrogantly said out loud. "Obviously, the great Cardinal must have been impressed with me to request my assistance in this matter."

Finally, with this assignment he felt there was a possibility of gaining respect from other clergy. He had been a chaplain for twenty years, but never felt as though fellow clergymen considered him to be on the same sanctimonious level as they were. At times, his distain towards them was difficult to hide. He would show them, by doing an outstanding job on this assignment. They would be compelled to invite him to be a member on the board of The Divine Council. He grinned sheepishly at the thought of having such power, totally oblivious to the fact that the Cardinal considered him a low-life, capable of being manipulated if there was any self-gratification involved.

The Council had quietly, but powerfully been controlling world religion since the time of the first Pope. Down through the ages the Council had assured the only teachings that reached their followers were the ones they approved. The original Council was formed to discredit what they considered pagan teachings by women. It had always been made up of twelve men in an effort to emulate the holy apostles. Over time, they had been so successful at controlling the teachings in Christianity that other religions had joined with them. Together they formed

The Divine Council, which discreetly manipulated the teachings in major religions throughout the world. Thus powerfully influencing basic beliefs, guiding the very lives of billions of followers.

"And now they request the help of Michael Santini! Ha!" Talking to himself, he stood straightening his uniform. "I'll show them I am worthy of this request."

Rachel had been at her computer writing for hours. Feeling extremely pleased with the progress of her book she decided to take a break and call her granddaughter to let her know she had emailed more chapters. She called Mariah's cell phone, but got her voicemail. She left a message telling her about the chapters and inviting her to dinner. James was also coming, and they hadn't all been together since the day of the funeral. Besides Rachel knew Mariah had been to the doctor's and was anxious to hear the latest update on her great-grandchild. She took her tea out onto the sun porch, while she read the New York Times.

A short time later the doorbell rang. Opening the door Rachel was quite surprised to see Mariah standing there with John Benson behind her.

Mariah kissed her on the cheek. "Sorry I didn't call Grand, but I needed to see you. You remember John?"

"Why yes of course, do come in. I was just having tea on the sun porch, please join me." Rachel led the way, gracious as ever.

After they were all settled comfortably with their tea she turned her attention to Mariah. "Is something wrong, dear?"

Mariah told her the story about the envelope she found in her car at the estate. It had turned out to be an eleven-page letter from someone who claimed to be her husband Joe's replacement. It went on and on about how he intended to take care of her, whether she wanted him to or not. And how he was watching her to be sure she was safe.

He said he was thrilled about the baby, insisting when Mariah eventually realized this was for her own good she would accept him as her husband.

"I'll let you read it later Grand, but that's the main idea of the letter. It's very frightening. This psycho just keeps rambling on about how I need him!"

John had been quiet up until now. "Mariah, tell her about the roses and the signature on the letter."

"Oh yes, this is really scary, Grand. He said he hoped I liked the yellow roses from him, for Joe. He was the one, Grand!" Mariah started to cry. She took the letter out of her purse and fumbled for the last page. She handed it to her grandmother.

The signature said, *Loving You Forever for Joe.*

Rachel frowned.

"I don't know if this person is dangerous, but perhaps we should report this to the authorities."

"No, Grand, I really don't want any more attention related to Joe's death." She stood and walked to the window. "Besides it would probably not be good for my business if it got out that some nut is stalking me." Mariah was adamant.

Before Rachel could disagree, John politely asked if he could say something. "I know this is none of my business, but I don't think the police will do anything about a letter or flowers. Think about it, whoever this is hasn't really broken any law. I have to agree with Mariah. It would only bring her unwanted publicity."

Rachel sighed. "Well maybe you are both right, but at least move back here, dear, so you won't be alone.

"I agree with your Grandmother, Mariah. You shouldn't be alone. How about if you bring me back to my car, and I follow you to your place? You can pack, and I'll follow you back here."

"Well, I don't know if all that's necessary . . ."

"Please Mariah, let John help you. I'll feel better. I wanted you to come to dinner this evening anyway. Will you join us John? My friend James will be here also."

"I would be delighted Rachel, thank you for my first social invitation in my new home town." John bowed slightly.

"Oh, John, the house. I forgot all about the offer. I'll call the clients as soon as we get back to the office. I can fax them the offer."

"It's okay, that's not important at the moment." He gave her his winning little boy smile.

"You've been too kind. We will get you that house."

She picked up her purse and kissed Grand. "Here's the rest of the letter if you want to read it while we're gone. We'll be back in a couple hours."

Rachel held on to Mariah's hand, looking at her seriously concerned, "Please dear, be careful."

Chapter 18

It was very effortless for Mariah to settle back into living at her grandmother's house. In fact standing out on the private beach, and looking back at the house she decided it was the perfect place to raise her child. After all, she had grown up here and had a wonderful time.

Realistically, she would need Grand's help with the baby so she could keep working. Right then Grand called to her from the deck, motioning for her to come back to the house. She walked slowly up the sand dune towards the wooden stairs. Her stomach, prominently showing her pregnancy now, was beginning to be a bit cumbersome. She didn't mind though, in fact she often thanked God for this miracle growing within her.

Grand was holding the phone towards Mariah, as she stepped onto the deck. "I think it's your office."

"Hello, Mariah Davidson speaking."

"Hello Mariah, it is so good to hear your voice again," a man's voice said very low.

"I'm sorry, who is this?"

"Come on, Mariah. Did you think I wouldn't know you moved into your grandmother's house? Didn't you believe my letter?"

Mariah raised her voice, "Who is this?"

There was a sick laugh on the other end of the line. "Don't play games with me. You know this is Joe. How is our baby?"

Rachel saw the terror on her granddaughter's face as Mariah yelled into the phone. "Don't you call me again you lunatic!" She was shaking as she sat down in the nearest chair.

Alarmed, Rachel called James, and because it was Sunday he was able to come right over. He checked Mariah over and found her blood pressure to be high.

"Mariah, this is not good. You need to take it easy for a day or so. I'll call your doctor tomorrow and let her know you have been under extra stress lately, but she will also recommend rest."

"Alright, Dr. James. I'll work from home for a couple days, but I will not let this nut control my life! That's exactly what he's trying to do." Mariah looked at the both of them defiantly, ready for an argument.

"I understand, dear, but right now you must think of what is best for you and your baby." James gently patted her protruding belly, giving her a fatherly smile.

"I'll check in with you ladies tomorrow to see how everything is. Rachel, be sure to lock the house up tight, and please set the alarm." He kissed each of them on the cheek and left.

Mariah did stay home for a few days. It was rather nice to lounge on the sun porch in the warmth of the summer breeze. It also gave her some time to read the most recent chapters of Grand's book. They were even more fascinating now that she knew who they were about, although she was still having some reservations about them being her ancestors. She was wondering what proof there was other than Grand claiming it to be true. It wasn't that she doubted her Grandmother, but it was just such an extraordinary story. It was difficult to understand why it would have been buried for the last two thousand years, or why it was dangerous to tell. Who would consider the story to be threatening? Mariah hoped these questions would be answered for her as the book evolved. She started to read and was immediately engrossed in this new chapter.

Chapter 19

In the days and weeks that followed the death of her husband, Mary remained close to home. She no longer traveled the countryside preaching. Instead, she found solace in helping her sister in the home.

Working in the home was a new experience for her. She was not familiar with all that had to be done to keep a house running smoothly. Her years as a temple priestess, had kept her on the road ministering to strangers. Although she loved what she was doing, Mary missed her family home, and would visit whenever she was in the area. Unfortunately, her visits were always short so Ruth insisted on treating her sister like a guest, instead of allowing her to help with the work. Now, that she was back she enjoyed sharing in the day-to-day chores, but Ruth was selectively choosing the jobs she gave to her.

"You must take care of yourself," she would say pointing to Mary's growing belly. "We want this baby to be strong and healthy."

She was happy to be working alongside her sister doing simple jobs. She needed time with family to help her heal and find her direction in life. Her husband's death had been such a shock. Suddenly, all their future plans were gone. Now she was going to have a child.

Mary looked at her belly, placing her hand at the top. "I don't know how I'm going to do this alone," she whispered as though talking to the child inside.

"You won't be alone." The voice startled Mary, and she quickly turned to see Ruth standing in the doorway. "We will always be here for you and the baby."

"I know you will. I was just feeling sorry for myself at the moment."

"Come, let's have something to eat. It is well past the noontime hour, you must be hungry," said Ruth as she gently placed her arm around her sister's waist leading her into the kitchen.

Mary smiled. She was hungry and was glad Ruth had suggested they eat. Her appetite was back to normal since the nausea had subsided causing her to put on weight. She could no longer tighten the braided cords she wore around her waist. There were times she would not wear the decoration, enjoying the freedom of loose fabric on her larger body. Tiredness was still an issue with the young mother-to-be. Once a high-energy priestess who rarely felt fatigue, she now found herself in need of a nap each afternoon to get through her day.

Some days, feeling refreshed from her nap, Mary would stroll out into the family vineyard. She loved the smell of the ripening grapes in the hot afternoon sun, at times she would pick a handful, enjoying their sweetness as she walked. Life seemed brighter when she was outside. She would breathe deeply in the warm air as though it was the source of her strength.

On just such an afternoon, Mary could see someone running to catch up with her. As the tall masculine figure came closer, she recognized her husband's friend Joseph.

"Ruth said you might be out here. I'm so glad I found you," he said trying to catch his breath.

"I am happy to see you, too"

Pointing to a nearby tree, Joseph suggested they sit and talk. "I'm getting too old to run like that. I need to rest."

A few deep breaths later, Joseph asked how Mary was feeling, and she proceeded to tell him how hard it was without her husband. He listened attentively, eventually she told him the news about the expected child.

"Mary, how wonderful. When is the baby due?

About the time of the winter solstice."

"And your family, are they excited?

"They are, and Ruth is already taking charge. She makes sure I don't work too hard and sees that I take good care of myself. Actually, it is nice to be part of the family on a daily basis. I have been a visitor for too long."

"Now that you are feeling better, do you think you will continue the ministry? The people still gather on the hillside, but there is no one to lead them. They ask for you, wondering if you will take your husband's place. They need you, Mary."

"No, Joseph, I'm not ready for that yet, I don't know if I ever will be. The memories are still too painful. I miss him too much.

Joseph heard the sadness in his friend's voice as he listened to her. Her eyes welled up, and her hand quickly went to her face to catch an escaping tear.

"I'm sorry. I didn't mean to upset you. Give it some thought. It might be what you need to help you move on in your grief."

"I will, but don't expect a miracle."

Joseph stood up and reached out his hands to help Mary to her feet. He hated seeing his friend's wife in so much anguish. He remembered happier times when her presence within the ministry added so much joy for her husband and the people.

"I'm here if you need me," said Joseph looking directly at Mary and holding her hand. "I made a promise to your husband to look after you, and I intend to keep it."

"Thank You, Joseph. You are a good man and I appreciate all your kindnesses. Good-bye," she said as she waved to the man walking briskly toward edge of the vineyard.

Several weeks later on a cool clear morning, before the sun had a chance to heat the earth, Mary left her home and strolled towards the seashore on the edge of the village. After breakfast she had begged off the morning chores and told a surprised Ruth she was taking a walk to the water's edge.

Mary had awakened feeling rested and refreshed, yet she felt unrest deep inside her. Although her family had been wonderful, and she was ever grateful for their love and support, she missed the independence of being on the road. She loved traveling to exciting new places where people were always so welcoming. She missed that part of her life.

The walk to the beach was not long, but Mary walked slowly. She stood erect with her head held high, taking in all the sights and sounds along the way, occasionally waving to someone she knew. For the first time in more than a month, she felt alive. The pain and loneliness of losing her husband seemed lessened for the moment.

The shoreline was deserted, and Mary breathed a sigh of relief in knowing that she was alone. As she stepped on to the beach, removing her sandals, she felt the sand between her toes, massaging the bottom of her feet.

The water's edge was rocky, and she cautiously made her way into the cool surf as it gently touched her toes. She stood ankle deep in the refreshing water, staring out onto the horizon.

Eventually she moved towards a long grouping of large rocks that ran from the beach into the water. Cautiously she walked across one then another until she came to a flat rock she could sit on. The water below gently slapped the rocks and her ankles, sometimes splashing water onto the hem of her garment.

Closing her eyes, she tilted her head back to feel the warmth of the sun on her face, while gentle breezes lifted stray curls from her brow. She felt happy thinking back on the wonderful times shared with her husband. Her left hand tenderly touched a gold pendant she wore around her neck. It had been his gift to her on their wedding day and she wore it always. His gift had become more precious with his passing.

As her finger traced the pendant's outline, Mary's thoughts drifted back to that day and remembered how playful her husband had been the night of their wedding.

Laughing, he had taken her hand and pulled her towards their room. Once inside, he encircled her with his arms pulling her tenderly to his body, smothering her with kisses tasting ever so faintly of wine.

"I love you," he whispered over and over as his warm lips savored the sweetness of her face and neck.

Her response was barely audible. Minutes passed before the two lovers breathlessly separated. He drew her to the edge of the bed never taking his eyes off of her. The lovers sat side by side as he gave her his gift.

"… the union of our love for all eternity," he whispered as he fastened it around her neck.

The pendant had been designed using the sacred almond-shaped symbol of the goddess repeated three times to form a triangular pattern that was entwined with an eternal circle.

Overwhelmed by his expression of love, she leaned forward and passionately kissed him on the mouth igniting her sacred fires, which burned long into the night.

Chapter 20

Mariah sat astonished at what she had just read in the manuscript. She could hardly wait for Grand to come home. All she could think of was the pendant her grandmother had always worn. Could it be the same one in the story, and was it the proof? Grand had always said it was a family heirloom, which was why she never took it off.

Mariah was already enthralled with the manuscript and now this, with the pendant. Putting the manuscript down, she leaned back closing her eyes. Thinking of how Joe died, she rubbed her stomach, feeling sad this child would never know its father. She couldn't help but identify with Mary who was in a similar situation, but in a very different and dangerous time. The telephone began ringing. Mariah got up to answer it, but she was moving slowly these days. The machine got it first, hearing the man's voice stopped her in her tracks.

"Mariah, I know you are there. You haven't been in your office since last week, which has me worried. I'm thinking I should come to the house and check on you." There was only the sound of breathing for a moment. "Are you ready to accept me yet? It is inevitable. I will take care of you. See you soon. Love you." Once again, self-satisfied, Peter hung up without identifying himself.

Mariah was panic-stricken. He was coming to the house. She didn't know what to do. My God, she thought, maybe he is dangerous. Grand won't be home for hours. I can't call the police, I don't want too. John will know what to do.

She got her cell phone, looked up his number and hit the call button. The phone kept ringing, his voicemail answered.

"John, it's Mariah. I just had a call from that psycho and, and … he says he's coming over here. I didn't know who to call, Grand is not home, but that doesn't matter … John please help me!"

Mariah was still panicked. She went around the house locking all the doors and widows. She pulled shades and closed the blinds. Just as she sat down to catch her breath in the kitchen the phone rang, startling her. She waited for the answering machine to pick it up. It was a woman's voice.

"Hi, Rachel. How's it going Hon? I was just calling to check on my favorite author. I'll try back later." Joan hung up. Mariah gave a sigh of relief.

But then the doorbell rang, someone started knocking heavily on the front door. Mariah grabbed a kitchen knife walking into the living room. "Who is it? Who's there?"

She could hear a man's voice, but did not know what he was saying. She was near hysteria now. She yelled, "I'm armed, and the police are on their way. You better leave me alone!" All she could hear was her own heart pounding.

"Mariah, It's me, John. It's John. Look out the window," he said very loudly, as he stepped back on the porch, so she could see him.

She gingerly lifted the curtain to peek out. It was John. She threw open the door and fell into his arms sobbing, still grasping the knife. He soothed her for a few minutes, gently taking the knife from her, as he guided her inside to the sofa.

"It's okay, it's okay now. Take some deep breaths." He sat next to her rubbing her back.

"Oh John, I was so scared. He said he was coming for me and …"

"Who said?" He looked puzzled.

"Didn't you get my message?" Now Mariah was confused.

"No. I was going to look at the outside of my new home. I stopped at the office, and Amy told me you were home. I thought you might want to go for a ride with me to the house."

"John, it was that psycho. I thought you were him at the door. Come in the kitchen, and I'll play the message for you. He listened intently to the rather threatening message.

He turned to her and hugged her. "I am so sorry, but I am really glad I stopped. Let him show up now! Do you recognize his voice?"

"No, not at all." She shook her head.

"Can I replay it? There's something familiar about his voice." John listened closely to the message three times. "I can't quite place it, but I know I have heard his voice before." He followed her out to the sun porch, and they sat down.

Rachel was very upset when she finally arrived home and heard what had happened. "I am having the number changed tomorrow, and it will be unlisted. Furthermore, from now on I don't want you to be alone anywhere, Mariah!" Mariah just nodded. She was exhausted from the stress of the day. John had left and she badly wanted to go to bed, but she had to hear Grand out.

Peter sat in his car with his head pounding. He had seen John leave, and he cursed him for even being there. He held his aching head, as he watched the lights go out one by one on the first floor of Rachel's house. He could wait. His time would come. In the meantime, Mariah would find two-dozen yellow roses waiting on her car in the morning.

Chapter 21

Joan listened impatiently to Chaplain Santini ramble on about Rachel's book. He was saying something about the people who had hired him having unlimited resources.

"Mr. Santini, Chaplain, I have another appointment, so could you please get to the point." Joan lied hoping he would just say what he wanted.

"Well, Ms. Hale, I am authorized to offer you a large sum of money for the manuscript prior to it's publication." He waited, feeling very smug and relishing the exhilaration from the sense of power he felt.

"Why in the world would anyone do that? Why do you want it?" Joan played dumb, but strongly suspected who was behind this offer. She also could guess why the Council would want a private preview of what promised to be a controversial book. They were always big on damage control, and this way they would be prepared to denounce Rachel's book, whether it was true or not.

"I am not at liberty to answer those questions Ms. Hale." Santini seemed impatient.

"But the manuscript is not even finished. I only have about half of it. Rachel is being very stubborn about letting me see more until it is finished. Creative license and all that ... authors can be extremely temperamental when it comes to their work." She gave an exasperated sigh, waiting for his response.

"How you obtain the manuscript is not my problem. I am offering you a six-figure amount, with half now for what you have. And the other half at whatever date you deliver the rest of the manuscript." He opened his briefcase and pulled out bundles of cash. Joan's eyes lit up with greed, as he placed them neatly on her desk.

"I need to think about this offer ... I have a reputation in the business ..."

"Yes, I know. That's why I thought we could do a confidential business transaction, but if you ..." He started to pick the money up.

Joan was quick to lean over the desk and put her hand over the money. "No, no, I think we can work something out that would be in both of our best interests." She smiled rather sinisterly, as she caressed the money. "I'll have the first installment of our deal delivered to you tomorrow."

Santini was wiping the sweat from his face, as usual. He gave her an equally evil grin revealing his tobacco-stained teeth, causing even Joan to cringe.

Behind closed doors, the Cardinal told the man on the other end of the phone he would be in possession of part of the requested material within the week. He did not know when the rest would be completed and delivered. But at least they would be able to ascertain if this woman's disclosure would threaten their doctrines in anyway. Also by being one step ahead of her the Council would be able to find a way to discredit her and the book before anyone considered believing it.

Rachel's book was coming along nicely. Writing it wasn't difficult, having heard the stories of her ancestors so many times from her own mother and grandmother. She just wanted to be sure to give all the details, as they had been related to her, while weaving them into a believable account of the way life must have been so long ago. It was very important the whole truth be revealed. Finally the world would know why the church had buried Mary Magdalene's story since the beginning. It would also be important for those responsible for the global oppression of women to finally admit it, although Rachel was not so naïve as to think that would happen easily. She realized she would have to brace herself for the deluge of negativity, which would be strategically released by the religious community in an attempt to discredit her book. But, as she had told Mariah, it was time for the world to hear the truth and know the great injustices men had propagated for the last two thousand years.

Mariah was beginning to understand. After her frightening experience with the stalker, Grand had been trying to stay closer, leaving Mariah alone as little as possible. Consequently, this had given them more time to discuss the legend and the book.

Rachel had told her that the gold pendant she wore was indeed the same symbol Jesus had lovingly bestowed upon his bride on their wedding day. She did not know if it truly was the same one, only that it had been passed down through the women in their family for centuries. The meaning behind the pendant was of great significance. It had come to symbolize the unification of the Sacred Feminine with the Divine Masculine—for all eternity.

The symbol represented what the church had denied for the past two thousand years, basically that Jesus considered Mary an equal in his dominion. She was his number one apostle; he fully trusted she would continue his teachings and carry the holy word to all who yearned to hear it. Certainly Mary had tried, but even then many followers of Jesus denounced her for one simple reason. She was a woman.

The apostles could not accept that a woman could be as powerful as they were. They had envied her closeness to Jesus when he was alive, but since he no longer walked among them they did not feel compelled to tolerate her extraordinary behavior. They were respectful of Mary because she was his widow and carried his child, but beyond that they had no patience for her acting as though she were an equal to them.

This was the very beginning of the denial of Mary's relationship to Jesus; as well the denunciation of women serving god in an equal capacity to men. Although not evident at the time, it would be the basis for the suppression of the Sacred Feminine in Christianity. Additionally it would be the origin of man's power within the church, and thus woman's lack of power. It would be the primitive foundation for the unwarranted inequalities dealt women down through time. The church's ill-gotten power would eventually have far reaching consequences in the oppression of women worldwide.

Rachel got so caught up in explaining the legend to Mariah she often lost track of time. She desperately wanted Mariah to understand the entire story. It was so important it be made public, and even more important people believe it.

"Grand, so this is a story that the Church knows about, yet has chosen to deny for some two thousand years?" Mariah asked incredulously.

"Yes, and you now understand how the truth could help restore the balance of power, benefiting women throughout the world once we are able to take our rightful place within sacred teachings again." Rachel leaned her head back in her chair, closing her eyes, imagining the possibilities.

Chapter 22

Mariah came home early from the office. They were redecorating the large room connected to her bedroom as the nursery. The contractors had finished painting and papering the day before, so Grand and her were going shopping for furniture and decorations today. It was very exciting. Together they had decided to decorate with a moon and star theme, using yellow, green and a touch of pink. It was a very neutral theme, which would be good for a girl or a boy.

After a long day of shopping they came home laden with bags and totally exhausted. Laughing about how much stuff they bought they dumped everything in the living room, to be unpacked later. Mariah decided if anyone gave a baby shower her child would need another room because one wouldn't be big enough.

Rachel put the teakettle on and started fixing them a light dinner. She made Mariah put her feet up to relax while she waited on her. Mariah picked up her cell phone. She had left it home intentionally, so she wouldn't be bothered by any business calls while baby shopping. She had four messages. She listened to one from John about the closing on his house, two more were from Amy at the office, but the last one sent a chill up her spine. It was the stalker.

"Grand, come listen to this message. It's him!" She handed the phone to Rachel.

The voice said, *"Mariah, my love, I have watched as you prepare for our child. I want to be part of the preparation, so I have left a few things for the both of you. We will meet soon. I feel it."*

"Sweetie, how would he get this number?"

"I don't know, maybe through the office. But he's watching me, watching the house. God, what did he leave?" She got up. Greatly agitated she hurried to the kitchen window checking for any sign of him.

They then opened the front door a crack to look out, but there was nothing on the porch. They had come in the side door and not seen anything there either.

"Never mind, Mariah. Let's take our dinner out to the sun porch. It looks like it will be a beautiful sunset." The sky was already pink and orange and reflecting off the water.

Mariah glanced out towards the sunset. "Oh my God, Grand, look!" She stood up and went to the door leading to the deck. The deck was piled high with baby toys, a highchair, a playpen, a carriage, a car seat, bags of baby clothes, and much more.

"He was on my deck? That's it Mariah, I am calling the police chief. You know David is a longtime friend. He'll keep this quiet." Mariah was speechless. She just nodded in agreement.

The chief listened intently, as the two women told the story of the stalker from the beginning when he had first sent the yellow roses. The chief did not think this man was dangerous, but did see a pattern building in his behavior. He was getting bolder with each incident. He felt this man would confront Mariah, and probably soon. Certainly, the chief did not want to take a chance of anything happening. Cautioning her not to go out alone, he promised to have a patrol car highly visible at both the house and her office. Rachel closed the door behind the chief, feeling a little better knowing the police were watching the house.

Chapter 23

The days seemed to fly by for Mariah. She was extremely busy at work and at home. In the past couple months, since John had closed on his home, he had enlisted her help in decorating. He claimed to be clueless when it came to decorating. Yet, the more they shopped for furniture and antiques the more Mariah realized he had exceptional, as well as expensive taste. He had hired a full time housekeeper, who also cooked for him. Three or four days a week he flew his private plane to New York on business, yet she still wasn't sure what he did. Whenever she mentioned money he would change the subject, so she let it go for a while. But she was curious.

The summer was winding down, however her real estate office was still very hectic. She was preparing her friend and fellow realtor, Amy, to take over the office while she was on maternity leave. The baby was due at the end of December, which worked out great for her taking five months or so off. She would return to work right when the summer season was starting again, their busiest time of the year.

Mariah still missed Joe terribly. She brought flowers to his grave often and talked to him about their child. It was coming up on the six-month anniversary of his death.

Sometimes it seemed like he died yesterday, and other times it felt like it had happened an eternity ago. The bigger her stomach became, the more she missed sharing this time with him. She was slowly starting to find enjoyment in small things again, but feeling quite guilty about it. She felt like it was wrong for her to be enjoying life when he had lost so much. She was constantly at odds with herself until one day at the cemetery. Standing in front of his heart shaped headstone she began crying, as she rubbed her stomach.

"Joe, I can't do this anymore, I just can't. You need to let go of me." She was sobbing now. "I need to go on with living, especially for our child's sake. I'll always love you, but I must go on." She turned and walked slowly towards her car, hardly able to see through her tears. She wanted to look back, but resisted. Ironically, had she turned around she would have seen a shadowy figure emerge from behind a tree, where he had been listening closely.

Mariah drove home feeling drained. She knew she was right, but it was so difficult to let go and move on. John had invited her to have dinner at his house Saturday night. He had purchased some new paintings he wanted her to see. They were becoming good friends, and she wanted to go. But she did not want to feel guilty, as though she were cheating on her husband.

When she arrived home, there was a note from Grand saying James had invited her to dinner. She would be home early and had left a casserole in the oven and a salad in the fridge. Mariah smiled, feeling fortunate to have such a loving person like Grand in her life. She was pleased that Grand was out with James. They had been together quite a bit lately; it was about time things got serious with the two of them. They had been good friends forever, or at least for as long as she could remember.

Going about getting her dinner out, she suddenly felt a familiar presence. She looked around the room, but saw no one. Still, she felt a very large presence quite near. She sensed a communication, although she did not actually hear a voice. It was almost like a telepathic message.

"It is all right. Joe understands. He understands. Everything is as it must be, for you and for him."

Then the comforting presence was gone as quickly as it had materialized. At first Mariah could not understand what had just taken place. She looked around the house to assure herself it was empty. Finally, sitting down to have her dinner, she thought about what had happened. Gradually, she started to realize she felt better, as though a weight had been lifted off her. A quiet feeling of peace came over her, and she smiled. It had taken her a little time to figure out the presence had been her guardian angel, but once she did it made perfect sense. They had met before. She remembered having the same feeling of comfort, as a child, after her parents were killed. Sampson had appeared to her in a dream, revealing his symbolic name for strength, and he had eased the pain in her heart then, also.

Not surprisingly, after what Mariah came to call her spiritual experience, her days seemed brighter. Her heart no longer ached as much for the past, instead she was filled with a joyful anticipation for the future with her baby.

In the office things were starting to slow down, so she had opted to start working from home part of the time. She would sleep later in the morning and take her time getting to the office, fully confident that Amy could handle the business. Showing up at the office at noontime on her birthday, she was absolutely astounded to find the whole front room filled with red roses. They were on every desk and counter. Amy met her at the door with a big smile, "Happy Birthday."

"Thank you, Amy. Who are these from?" she asked anxiously.

"I thought you would know. A man delivered them early this morning when I first opened. He didn't say much, but he did leave a card." Amy pointed to Mariah's desk.

She hesitantly walked to her desk, fearing what the card might say. Her name was written on the envelope, and she immediately recognized it as the same handwriting that had been on the letter. She froze.

"Mariah, are you okay? Mariah?" Amy had her arm around her now. "Mariah, sit down." She poured her a glass of water. "Sip this Hon, you don't look well."

She took a sip of the water. "Amy, what did this man look like?" She still held the unopened envelope in her hand.

"I really didn't pay much attention to him. I figured he was just the delivery guy. Why?"

"This is the nut that was stalking me a couple months ago. He disappeared when my Grandmother called the police in. They patrolled our house regularly and even parked out in front at times. He never made contact again after that, so we assumed he was gone. But … now …" Mariah looked fearful, as she surveyed the dozens of roses.

"Are you going to open the card?" Amy was frightened to think this weirdo had been alone in the office with her.

"Yes." Mariah picked up her letter opener and slit the envelope. The front of the card said, "To My Beloved Wife." She held her breath as she opened the card and read the verse out loud. It was all about how much he loved her and would be with her for the rest of her life. He had written a note in it also.

"My dearest Mariah, I know you are ready to get on with your life, especially for our baby. You are finally ready to move on, and I am still here. You cannot deny this because I heard you say you must go on. Did you notice the roses have gone from yellow to red? The red roses are the new symbol of our love. We will be together soon! Happy Birthday, Loving you Forever, Joe."

Realizing he must have been at the cemetery spying on her shocked her at first. But, she suddenly felt more anger than fear. She slammed the card on the desk. "This crackpot is not going to ruin the birth of my child or frighten me anymore!" Mariah dialed Grand's number to tell her what had happened, but not before she angrily threw every last rose in the trash.

Chapter 24

John had asked Mariah if he could take her out to dinner for her birthday. She was flattered, especially when he insisted on picking her up as though it were a real date. He brought her to an exclusive country club in the next town where he recently joined for the golf course, but had heard the dining was excellent. He told her he thought she might be more comfortable away from the town busybodies, and they both laughed recalling that day in the office with Helen.

John was the perfect gentleman, opening doors for her and holding her chair. He even offered her his sport coat against the chilly October night. He had reserved their own private dining room and had it filled with candles and flowers. There was a lovely centerpiece with a happy birthday sign on the table. The romantic atmosphere took Mariah completely by surprise.

"Why, John, this is lovely." She looked at the flowers instead of him, feeling a bit shy.

He took her hand. "Mariah, I wanted to make your birthday special for a number of reasons. You are an exceptional lady, and it means a lot to me that you have become such a special friend. With all you've been through you still opened your heart to a stranger. You have made me feel as though I have truly come home." John lifted his glass of wine to her. "To treasured memories and a blossoming future, happy birthday, Mariah."

She lifted her glass of water and clinked it with his glass. She felt like a schoolgirl on her first date, blushing and giggling.

"Thank you, John." She looked into his eyes. "I want you to know your friendship has meant so much to me. Other than Grand, there are few people I am comfortable with talking about Joe and all that has happened." Feeling the familiar lump in her throat she quickly took a sip of water. "Besides, when else would I ever get to decorate such a fabulous house on an open budget?" They both laughed and the seriousness of the moment was quickly lightened.

They dined slowly, enjoying each other's company, getting to know each other even better. Her curiosity finally got the best of her. "John, what do you do for work? I mean, I know it's not my business, nor do I want to pry, but you are obviously financially comfortable." She immediately felt embarrassed she had asked.

"It's all right, Mariah. I know you must be curious. I just don't like to tell people until I know they are truly my friends." John poured himself another glass of wine. "I work in the financial part of my family business. I inherited the business when my dad died a few years ago. I was in the service doing what I wanted to do, so a trusted colleague of my father's was overseeing the company until I returned."

"What kind of business is it?"

"Frozen food products. Not very exciting, but it has done well since my grandfather founded it some fifty years ago." John gave her his endearing schoolboy smile, which never failed to touch her heart.

Slowly it dawned on Mariah. She looked at him with disbelief. "Do you mean Benson Frozen Foods is your company?"

John laughed at the look on her face. "Yes."

Just then a group of servers crowded into the small room with a birthday cake and sang to Mariah. They didn't see one of the servers in the back of the group, or they may have recognized him.

Peter couldn't believe his luck to have Mariah dining where he worked. He watched and waited for them to emerge from their private dining room. When they finally came out into the lobby John left her standing alone, while he went to the men's room. Peter was shaking with the anticipation of being so close to her. He walked by her carrying a tray, intentionally bumping into her he dropped the tray, with a loud clatter.

Immediately he took her arm, thrilled at the feel of her flesh in his hand. "Excuse me! I am so sorry, are you okay?" He now held both of her arms, as though he were concerned.

"I'm fine, thank you. You barely touched me." He did not let go of her.

"Are you sure?" His heart was pounding with her so near. He inhaled the scent of her perfume deeply, and it took all of his self-control not to pull her into his arms.

Just then John appeared at her side. Peter let go of her and bent down to clean up the tray. "What's going on?"

"It's nothing, John. Just a small accident, I'm fine."

He looked at the server. "Peter?"

The server looked up. "Why hello, John, what a surprise to run into you and your friend." He gave an insincere laugh, as he nervously stood up.

"This is Mariah Davidson. Don't you remember her from Joe's funeral?" John was puzzled at running into Peter in this area. "Are you living here in New England now?"

Peter was totally focused on Mariah. "Why of course I remember you." He offered his hand to shake and covered hers completely with his other hand when she responded.

"How are you, Mariah?"

She pulled her hand away. "Fine, thank you."

He briefly explained to them that he had relatives in town and had decided to try living on the East coast.

On the drive home they talked about how odd it was to run into Peter, and how strange he seemed. Mariah had felt very uncomfortable with the way he kept touching her. She recalled feeling the same way at the funeral, with his clammy touch. They changed the subject to what a lovely evening it had been. She thanked him again for making her birthday special with all he had done. As they pulled up in front of Grand's house, he surprised her by for her taking a small gift-wrapped box from the back seat.

"Oh John, you didn't have to. You've already done so much." He put a single finger gently to her lips.

"I wanted to do this for you, happy birthday." He gestured for her to open it.

She opened the present to find a beautiful gold charm bracelet inside. It had two charms on it. One was a three dimensional little house and the other was a heart outlined in diamonds.

"It's beautiful, thank you, put it on my wrist."

He fumbled with the bracelet a little, but finally got it latched. "Now let me explain. The house represents my home, which you found for me and will always be connected to. The heart represents many things, but there is an inscription on it you can read when you go in. It says it best." He leaned over gently kissing her forehead.

John was elated with the evening, feeling that everything had gone well with Mariah. Driving home now, thinking about her, he hoped he had not gone too far with the bracelet. He was trying to move slowly, although he knew he was falling in love with her. It was too soon, she was still grieving, and she had the arrival of the baby to think about. He could be content with their close friendship until Mariah was ready for something more. He had never met anyone so worth waiting for. He fully believed she was his soul mate.

There was something nagging him about the evening. He kept thinking about running into Peter. It really was not so odd Peter had relocated, after all so had John. Maybe it was something Peter had said. John couldn't quite put his finger on it.

Mariah quietly turned out the lights on the way to her bedroom. She turned the lamp on in her room and held the bracelet under it. It really was lovely. She turned the heart over, inscribed on the back was the date and three words, "To the Future." She smiled. That certainly left it wide open to interpretation. She snuggled into bed thinking about the evening. She fell asleep thinking what a sweet man John was.

Chapter 25

Rachel waited impatiently for Joan to arrive at her home. The agent was still pressuring her to hurry with finishing the book. It was Rachel's idea for them to meet today to discuss a reasonable deadline. The meeting was mainly to stop the agent's harassing phone calls. Rachel sat in her study reading the most recent part of her manuscript. She printed out the last few chapters for Mariah, wanting to keep her up to date with the progress of the story, so it would not be too much for her to absorb at once. It was such a complex tale it seemed easier to answer Mariah's questions and offer explanations a section at a time; so far it had worked out splendidly. The printer was stilling running when the doorbell rang. Rachel greeted Joan showing her into the study. She removed her coat and warmed her hands at the fireplace.

"Looks like an early winter this year with it this cold already." She rubbed her hands together.

"Yes, it is rather chilly for this time of year. Would you like something hot to drink?" Rachel asked taking her coat.

"Tea would be wonderful, if it's not too much trouble." She seemed unusually pleasant.

Rachel smiled. "I'll be right back, make yourself comfortable."

Joan listened to the footsteps fade down the hallway before she reached into her purse. She walked over to the computer and plugged in the flash drive. Touching the mouse she couldn't believe her good fortune to have the document she wanted to copy already open. She instantly copied the manuscript to the memory stick and unplugged it. When Rachel returned she had no clue her manuscript had been electronically stolen.

"I've made you an outline of my work so far and my future writing." She handed it to her. "As you can see I have a projected timeline for when each part of the book will be finished. I am hoping this will be satisfactory, so you won't feel the need to constantly pressure me." She eyed the agent questioningly.

Joan slowly sipped her tea as she perused the timeline. "Okay Hon, I can live with this schedule, as long as you can meet the December deadline."

"The only thing, which could possibly slow me down would be the early arrival of my great-grandchild, and even that would only be a temporary diversion." She waited for a negative response, yet Joan seemed to know better than to say anything against Mariah or the baby.

The agent winked at her saying, "It's a deal! I promise not to call more than once a week, just to check in with you."

They shook hands and agreed it was a deal.

"Listen Rachel, while I am here I need to ask you a couple things about your story. It is an amazing story, but I just don't know if people will believe it is true. Do you have anything to substantiate the legend?"

Rachel thoughtfully fidgeted with her pendant. "There is my pendant, but it has never been authenticated. I don't know if it is the original or a copy. There is one other item of proof, which was passed to me with the pendant." She was very hesitant to confide in Joan.

"It is terribly important to the validity of your book that we have some kind of tangible evidence. If you can show me proof your ancestral bloodline truly descends from Jesus and his wife, Mary, then I will leave it to your discretion whether to publicize the proof or not."

"This is not something that has ever been seen or divulged outside of my family, so I will have to think about it, Joan." Rachel was frowning and looking especially serious now.

It was taking every ounce of self-control Joan could muster to not appear excited or over anxious to obtain this secret evidence. Undisclosed proof Jesus was married and did have a family would be worth a fortune. She thought no, it would actually be priceless. "Of course Hon, you just take your time, and think about it." She rose to leave. "I'll call you."

Rachel went back into the study and sat in front of the fireplace. Contemplating her conversation with Joan and the difficult decision, which now lie in front of her. The secret had not been shared outside of the family in the past two thousand years, as far as she knew. It seemed like a terribly heavy decision to be the person to disclose this proof to the world. Yet, on the other hand she wanted the legend to be believed. The truth did need to finally be known, for the sake of all women.

Chapter 26

As Rachel gathered the chapters she had just printed for Mariah she dropped some of the papers. She picked them up and sat by the fireplace to put them back in order. The last chapter caught her attention, and she started reading it again.

It wasn't long before Mary's many visits to the shore caught the attention of the local townspeople. Although they never interrupted her reflective time on her favorite rock, they would stop to say hello as she left the warm sandy beach. Gone was her need to avoid people for fear of their questions. She now enjoyed talking to those she grew up knowing and those she had ministered to with her husband. All had been concerned with her well being. They cared greatly and it showed in their voices.

Not far from the beach, a young woman waited on the roadside one day hoping to meet up with Mary as she returned to her home. Ashera had been a handmaiden when Mary had been in service to the goddess. She too left the temple to follow the young Rabbi that Mary later married.

"Mary," she called as she saw her friend approach.

Mary smiled as she recognized her long time friend and they embraced. "It is so good to see you, Ashera. How are you?"

"I am well, and am happy to see you."

"I'm on my way home. Why don't you come along and stay for dinner. I am sure Ruth would love to see you, and we can have some time to talk."

The invitation was gratefully accepted, and Ruth warmly received both women when they entered the house. After enjoying the evening meal, Mary and Ashera walked into the gardens to enjoy the cool evening air and to talk. Ashera was glad to be alone with her. She had noticed Mary's loose clothing, she guessed the rumor of her being with child must be true. When asked, Mary confirmed the upcoming event, and her friend was overjoyed.

The women had much to talk about and time went by quickly. Eventually Ashera made mention of Mary taking over her husband's ministry.

"Joseph asked me the same question several weeks ago, and I couldn't give him an answer. So much has changed, and now I am going to have a baby. A part of me would really like to preach again, but I wonder if the crowds would respond to me as their teacher without my husband present."

"Of course they would," responded Ashera. "Not a day goes by that they don't inquire about your return. They love you as they loved him, Mary. Why don't you come and see?"

After much encouragement, Mary agreed to meet Ashera the next morning, and together they would go to the hillside where people met and prayed. She was nervous as she set off from her home to meet her friend. Many questions went through her head about her capabilities to lead her husband's followers. Once confident, she now had doubts. Everything had changed. She had changed. The closer they came to the hillside, the slower she walked, breathing deeply to calm her nerves.

Mary could see a small group of people talking to each other, and she breathed more easily knowing that expectations would be less in a smaller crowd. As Ashera and Mary set foot on the base of the hillside, they were instantly noticed and some of the people came to greet them with smiles on their faces.

"Welcome, Mary."

"Thank you, Ashera, for bringing Mary to us."

"We are happy you have come to join us." Were some of the many comments and greetings the young women were met with.

It was not long before Mary felt comfortable walking amongst the people, many of whom she was able to call by name. Those she did not know were pleased to meet her and greeted her warmly as the Rabbi's widow.

"Mary, would you lead us in prayer this morning?" an older woman asked.

"No, please, I have just come to be among you, as Ashera asked."

Truthfully, Mary had not prayed for months since her husband had been killed. She could not find it in her heart to pray to the father who would let such a horrific thing happen. Mary was angry with the god of her husband. How could she lead prayers when there were none in her heart? Still, others asked as the crowd came nearer and surrounded her in expectation of her words. She stood at the center, eyes closed and head bent, searching for words that would not come. For what seemed like an eternity, all stood silently and reverently as they waited for her to pray. They were a patient and loving crowd, and Mary did not want to disappoint them, yet she struggled with what to say.

Suddenly, she uttered the one word she had refused to acknowledge for months. "Father," she called. "Bless the people who have come to worship," and the words came forth as she relaxed and led the people in prayer. Mary was surprised that the longer she prayed, the more her heart was open to praying. She was overwhelmed by the flood of emotions that overcame her. She felt more confident in her abilities, and could feel the sincerity of the people who prayed with her.

When prayers had subsided, Mary sat and visited with the people. They had been meeting several times a week and hoped she would join them. That morning on the hill, with her leading, had been the answer to their prayers.

"Mary, please tell us about your husband's last days. We have missed him," said an old man sitting nearby.

Mary thought for a few minutes. Except for her sister Ruth, she had not talked to anyone about that last week. The events were still too painful to talk about. But then she thought of the Passover meal they had shared with his apostles, and she started talking to the people gathered around her. They sat quietly listening, eager to hear every word she had to say.

"Earlier in the day, two of the apostles had been sent into the city to secure a room, and see to preparations for the Passover meal. Several women helped in gathering and preparing the foods that were enjoyed by our friends and family that evening in an upper room, which was comfortably furnished with large sitting cushions and warmed with the glow of oil lamps.

Along with the twelve apostles, we had asked his mother, Mary, to also join in the feast. We prayed the solemn prayers of our ancestors and then enjoyed the foods brought before us. Conversation flowed freely among us as we leisurely sat in a circle around the food. As I sat by my husband's side, I watched his face and could see how he enjoyed his friends' company. His hearty laugh was often heard in response to their conversations."

As she told the story, Mary privately remembered how her husband had often touched her hand throughout the evening as a loving gesture. She had smiled at him in return. Expressions of their love for each other were a daily part of their lives, as natural as breathing. She missed these intimate moments, but would treasure them in her heart always.

"When the meal was over, my husband quieted his guests and said to them, 'I have eagerly desired to eat this Passover with you before I suffer, for, I tell you, I shall not eat it again until there is fulfillment in the kingdom of God.' Then he took a cup, gave thanks, and said, 'Take this and share it among yourselves; for I tell you that from this time on I shall not drink of the fruit of the vine until the kingdom of God comes.' Then he took the bread, said the blessing, broke it, and gave it to each of us, saying, 'This is my body, which will be given up for you; do this in memory of me.' And likewise the cup after they had eaten, saying, 'This cup is the new covenant in my blood, which will be shed for you.'" (Luke: 22,14-20)

With these words, Mary paused in silence remembering the solemn part of their evening. As with the crowd before her, the occupants of the room had listened in silence as her husband had spoken.

The stillness was broken by the sound of a young woman asking Mary, "What did he mean by do this is memory of me?"

Mary explained further, "he asked each of us present that evening, in his memory, to share his body and blood, in the form of bread and wine, with those who believed in him and his word."

"Will you do this for us?" continued the woman.

Mary pondered the request and hesitated. She had come to the hillside only to observe. Yet, as she looked at each of the eager faces before her, she could see how much the people wanted her as their minister. Not wanting to disappoint them, and with her newly regained confidence, she said, "Yes." Plans were then made for the breaking of the bread at their next gathering.

When the crowd broke up, Mary lingered behind with some friends she had not seen in a long time. The women were about the same age, with some approaching their thirtieth year, as was she. All were married with children and were excited when Mary told them she was expecting. Jokes about her changing figure brought laughter as the women hugged her. Mary had not laughed so hard in a long time, and it felt good to be among such warm and caring women. She had much to tell Ruth on her return home early that afternoon.

Rachel finished reading and took her glasses off, laying the manuscript on the desk. Opening a drawer, she removed the key from where it had long been hidden, it belonged to an old safe deposit box. The decision was made. She must share the proof. Her book must be believed.

Chapter 27

Mariah got back to the office from a showing late in the afternoon. Amy had already left to pick her little girl up from school. Mariah checked her messages. John had left her a message to call him as soon as she could. She was checking her email when the bell on the door rang. A man entered, looking over his shoulder, as though someone might be behind him. When he looked back in her direction, she was surprised to see it was Peter.

"Why hello, Peter! What a surprise to see you again so soon."

"Hello, Mariah. It's especially nice to see you again." He walked over to her desk and sat down. "John told me you were in real estate, so I thought you might help me find a house. I saw one for sale I would like to see today if possible."

"I'll be glad to help you Peter, although it's kind of late to see a house today. What house are you interested in?"

"It's on Shore Drive, it looks empty."

Mariah thought for a moment. "I don't know of any vacant houses in that area. I'm sure I would have noticed since I live near there."

"Take a ride with me, and I'll show it to you. It's just what I am looking for!" He grinned nervously fidgeting with a paperweight on her desk.

She hesitated for a second. "Okay, I was getting ready to close up anyway. I'll follow you in my car since it is right near where I live." Mariah turned the computer off and clicked the answering machine on. He watched her, relieved that he would not have to use force.

Peter held the door for her. Then unconsciously stood jingling his keys, as he grew impatient, waiting for her to lock up. She followed closely behind him wondering what house could be for sale, and why she wouldn't have known about it.

John was frantically knocking on Rachel's front door. When she opened it he did not offer his usual polite greeting, but peered past her, while anxiously asking if Mariah was home.

"She's at the office John. What's wrong?"

"Rachel, there's no time to explain. Do you still have the message the stalker left on your machine?"

"Yes, I believe we saved it, come in." Rachel led the way to the answering machine.

John played the message, listening carefully. "That is him! I am sure of it!"

"Who, John?" Rachel was getting upset.

"It's Peter, the guy that was in Iraq with me and Joe. We saw him at the country club the other night, and the last thing he said was he would see us soon. It's the same thing he said in his message! It's been bothering me since then, but I just put it together."

Rachel had the phone in her hand. "We must tell Mariah. What if he approaches her? She'll think he's a friend."

"I already left her a message at the office to call me. Try her cell phone!"

"Here John you call. I am too nervous." She pushed the phone towards him with shaking hands.

Peter's car stopped in front of the old Stonington mansion. Mariah parked behind him, very curious now. There was a hand made "for sale" sign on the front lawn, and there were lights on in the house.

"See, Mariah, isn't it perfect?" He opened her door, took her arm almost pulling her out of the car. He walked a few steps toward the front door.

"Peter, I know the people who live here. This home has been in their family for decades, and I don't think they would sell it. Anyway, we can't just knock on their door."

"Sure we can. Come on!" He pulled her a little too forcefully. She was becoming apprehensive; his behavior was starting to be weird, yet it had not dawned on her that she might be in danger.

Back in Mariah's car her cell phone was ringing relentlessly. John would get her voicemail, hang up, and hit redial over and over. He had already left an urgent message about Peter, but the longer he could not contact her the greater his concern became.

Chapter 28

Peter guided her up the steps to the massive front door. He lifted the knocker and rapped three times, holding her by the arm the whole time. He grinned at her saying, "Well, I guess no one is here to show you the house, so I will!" He opened the door and pulled her inside.

Mariah couldn't believe what he was doing. "But, Peter ... you can't. I mean we can't just walk into this house!"

Oblivious to her objections, he was now closing the door and locking the deadbolt. He turned to her with a crazed look in his eyes. "But, darling, this is our new home. I can't wait to show you the nursery!"

Stunned Mariah took a step back. "Peter, it's you? You're the one that has been stalking me?"

"Now let's drop the pretense, Sweetheart. I've simply been courting you from a distance until we could be together. And now that we are home you can call me Joe." He took her hand and kissed it.

She was so shocked by what was happening it took her a minute to compose herself. She pulled away from him. "I need to leave." She tried to walk past him, but he blocked her way.

With his face inches from hers, he became excited. "Now, now, Mariah, it's been a long day, and you should rest. Come sit down." Turning her in the opposite direction and putting his arm around her, he almost carried her into the dining room.

She could hardly grasp what was happening. There must have been a hundred candles lit throughout the room. The table was set for two with china and crystal, and there were so many vases of red roses the air was heavy with their scent. He seated her on the side of the table away from the doorway. Then pouring her some water he offered a platter of cheese and fruit. She was really frightened, not being sure how mentally unbalanced he was. She kept thinking about her baby. She did not want to do anything that might provoke Peter into harming her, so she decided to play along by pacifying him until she could figure out how to escape. With her hand shaking she took a piece of cheese, and forcing a smile she thanked him.

Peter leaned over close to her inhaling her perfume. She could feel his hot breath on her neck, and it took all of her self-control to contain her repulsion. "As soon as you feel revived I want to show you our baby's room." He was extremely excited.

Mariah quickly said she was ready, hoping he might let her leave once he had shown her around. He guided her from behind as they climbed the stairs, caressing her upper arms as he gently moved her along. All she could think was she had not told anyone where she was going or with whom. There was no help coming. If he would not let her leave, she would have to figure out how to escape herself, without endangering her baby. Peter was babbling about redecorating the house, so she nodded, pretending to be interested. He made a sweeping motion throwing open the door to the nursery.

"I wanted a grand nursery fit for a king, or a queen as it may be. Only the best for our child!" He took her hands and forcefully pulled her into the room. "Do you approve my, sweet?"

Trying to act normal she replied, "Why yes, Peter, it is lovely." Her heart was pounding harder with her growing fear as she began to realize that he was insane.

"Darling, don't try to make me jealous by calling me by an old boyfriend's name." He leered at her repulsively, placing both of his hands on her stomach and rubbing it. Involuntarily she stiffened at his touch, which immediately enraged him. She felt a foreboding chill pass through her whole being, recalling all the sick things he had said in his letters and calls.

Chapter 29

Rachel had just hung up from the police chief. She told him Mariah was two hours overdue getting home, and also that they suspected Peter was the stalker. The chief was putting out an alert for Mariah's car. Meantime, Amy was meeting John at the office to see if they could find any clue as to where Mariah might have gone. Amy booted up the computer, while John rummaged through papers on Mariah's desk. "Call John" was written on her pad, so she had gotten his message. On the same piece of paper "Shore Dr." was scrawled with a couple question marks after it.

"Amy, does Shore Drive mean anything to you?"

Amy thought for a moment. "Not off hand. Let me see if there are any listings there." She turned to the computer and did a search. "Nothing, I don't find any homes for sale there. But John maybe there's house she went to list on Shore Drive."

"Good thinking, Amy. I'll drive over there and see if I can find her. Could you call Rachel, and tell her to pass the information on to the police?"

Amy nodded. "Consider it done. Hurry up, go!"

Still angry, Peter led Mariah across the hall to the master bedroom suite. Having an increasingly difficult time acting calm and composed, she was terrified of what he may have in mind, yet had not seen an opportunity to escape. She thought the safest thing to do was to play along until there was an opportunity to get away or signal for help. Thinking about her cell phone in the car, she really regretted not having called Grand to say where she was going. No one would have a clue where she was.

"Mariah? Are you listening?" Peter was looking at her. "I have a lovely surprise for you in your private dressing room." He put his hand out to show her the way.

John drove as fast as he could through town, following Amy's directions to Shore Drive, repeatedly trying Mariah's cell phone, but still getting no answer. His concern was growing, knowing she never went this long without her phone, or returning her calls. He finally turned onto Shore Drive. It was a wealthier section of town, and although the houses were large and expensive, most of them were only summer homes. Amy had told him most of the houses would already be closed up for the season. John slowed the car, it was beginning to get dark out. He felt an increasing sense of urgency to find her before nightfall. The whole street seemed deserted. Many houses had shuttered windows and shrubs wrapped in protective fabric to guard against the ocean's wrath through the winter. Suddenly he noticed lights on in an oceanfront house up ahead. He turned his headlights off, as he quietly rolled up in front of the property. There were two cars in the driveway. One of them was Mariah's.

Mariah felt panic rising in her chest. Peter had brought her into a dressing area. There, laid out on a lounging sofa was a white full-length lace and satin negligee with a matching robe. The panic was constricting her throat now. Suddenly she had an idea that might save her, or least buy her some time. She would pretend to be in labor, but she had to be convincing.

John could hear his heart pounding as he peered into Mariah's car. He could see her phone on the seat. He dialed 911 on his own phone. Speaking softly he instructed the operator to tell the chief he was at this address and had found Mariah's car. He quietly sneaked around the house trying to see in the windows in an attempt to assess the situation. He froze in his tracks when he saw the dining room. Looking at all the candles, roses, and the two place settings he knew it had to be the psycho, Peter.

Mariah was starting to breath heavy, so he would notice. She was also rubbing her protruding belly. She said, "Pete … er … Joe, I really need to sit down. I think all the excitement has been too much for me." She tried to smile convincingly.

Peter took her arm and brought her back into the bedroom. Sitting her on the edge of the king size bed he caressed her face, slowly letting his hand drift down her neck to her breasts. She stiffened in reaction to his touch, but he seemed not to notice. He quietly asked if he could get her anything, never taking his eyes from her breasts, as he firmly cupped both them in his sweaty hands. She felt the baby kick hard, as if in protest.

"I could really use some ice water," she whispered, as though she were weak. He hurried out of the room. Mariah got up quietly and looked out the bedroom door. She didn't know how to get out of the house without him seeing her. She couldn't just walk down the stairs they had come up. He would come back that way. Going back into the room, she looked out the window. It was dark out now. She couldn't see anything.

John saw a figure briefly in an upstairs window and thought it was Mariah, but couldn't be sure. He was hoping the police would get there quickly. He was on the back deck when he ducked down because someone came into the kitchen. He could see it was a man, so he slipped back to the side of the house throwing a stone at the window where he had seen the woman. Nothing. He threw another one. Someone was opening the window now.

"Mariah, Mariah?" John whispered loudly.

"Yes, help me, please." She couldn't see him, but knew it was John's voice. "Help me, he is …" Her voice faded out.

"Mariah?" John whispered again and listened. She had turned from the window. Now he heard a man's voice, so he kept quiet.

"What are you doing, Mariah?" Peter asked as she turned from the window. He handed her the ice water, eyeing the window suspiciously.

"Oh, I felt faint and wanted some fresh air." She sipped the water trying to look calm. "I do feel better."

"Okay, good." He closed the window locking it. Turning, he scrutinized her for a moment, as a sickly smirk spread across his face. "Well, then I think it's time for you to model your new lingerie for your husband."

Mariah did not know what to do. She had to stall him, fearful of what he may have in mind. Out of patience, he pushed her roughly into the dressing room. "Do you need me to help you?" He fondled her arm. Mariah jerked her arm away without thinking until it was too late. He was angered by her obvious rejection. His eyes narrowed and his face became flushed.

Peter pointed to the negligee, "Put it on. Now!"

Mariah moved slowly, pretending to obey. "May I change in private?" She was terrified. Once again she felt panic rising within her. Seeing no escape now, she silently asked her guardian angel to protect her and the baby.

Arrogantly, he sat down on the vanity bench and sneered, "I prefer to watch, or even help if I choose."

She could not think of any more ways to stall, so slowly she started to undress with her back to him. She thought she would be sick when she heard him begin breathing heavily and didn't dare look at him. He suddenly jumped up, grabbed the lace nightgown, and roughly put it over her head, pulling it down the length of her body. The pounding of Mariah's heart was so loud in her ears she was sure he could hear it. He now held the matching robe up, motioning her to slip into it. As she did, his arms surrounded her, and his hands enveloped her breasts. He began kissing her neck, telling her how happy they would be. Finally, losing all control she jerked away from him.

"Please, please don't hurt me, don't hurt my baby." She begged.

He was taken aback by her plea. "Mariah, darling, I would never hurt our baby. I love you and our unborn child. Come." He led her into the bedroom, seating her on the bed. "Let me show you the love I hold for you."

He calmly started to unzip his pants just as someone started knocking on the front door. Obviously agitated Peter told her to stay there, locking the door as he left. Mariah immediately tried to force the door open and started beating on it, while yelling for help.

As Peter got to the bottom of the stairs, someone pounded forcefully on the front door saying it was the police. He looked around frantically, realizing he must be in trouble, but not quite comprehending why. Confused, he made a dash for the sliding door in the kitchen, acting crazed like a cornered animal. He dashed out onto the deck, something hit him hard in the back of the head, and he crumbled into a heap.

John yelled for the police chief, just as two officers came around the back of the house. They had their weapons drawn, so John raised his hands dropping the piece of wood he had hit Peter with. The chief was right behind them and told them to cuff the guy that was down. John rushed inside calling for Mariah. She was still banging on the bedroom door and yelling for help when he got upstairs.

"Mariah, it's John," he told her as he approached the door to unlock it.

He opened the door and wrapped his arms around her. "Are you all right? Did he hurt you?" He held her at arms length examining her tear stained face. Noticing what she was wearing he wrapped his coat around her.

"Oh, John I was so scared. No, he didn't hurt me, but I don't want to think what may have happened if you hadn't found me." She leaned up against his strong chest and began to sob. John held her, as the months of accumulated fear drained from her. Completely exhausted Mariah looked up at him.

"Please, can we just go home?"

Chapter 30

Mariah was put on complete bed rest for a week after her horrifying experience. She was in her eighth month, and her doctor was concerned about the strain she had been under. Rachel doted on her. She brought her meals in bed or only allowed her to be up long enough to take a meal by the fireplace.

John visited almost daily, often staying for dinner. He brought her flowers or little things for the baby. Mariah found him endearing. She was becoming very attached to him and found herself thinking about him quite often. On the days he couldn't visit she anxiously awaited his phone call, which frequently lasted for an hour or more. She still missed Joe terribly at times, but John's friendship lessened the deep aloneness she had been feeling since Joe's death.

She was able to read more of Rachel's book while on mandatory bed rest. Mary's story was growing more complex with each chapter. And the more complex her story became, the clearer the reasons for the church's denial of her became. She was obviously powerful. Furthermore, Jesus not only allowed this, but encouraged it. Had the church not denied the true story of Mary and her husband, women would have clearly had equal power within the church, as well as their communities. How very different the world would be Mariah thought, as she picked up the next chapter and began to read eagerly.

Chapter 31

The child within her was growing, and Mary was finding her once extensive wardrobe becoming limited. Her robes that used to fit her tall slim body were becoming tighter by the day, making it impossible to wear most of her clothes.

"You are going to need some looser clothes made, Mary," commented Ruth one day as her sister complained about not having anything to wear.

Mary smiled at her practical sister. "Look," she said as she ran her hand over her belly from top to bottom, creating an arc to proudly emphasize her new shape. "The child is healthy and grows bigger each day. No wonder I have trouble walking as fast as I used to. I find myself winded at the smallest incline."

"You are nearing your time, and it won't be long before you will be holding the child in your arms."

Mary barely heard her sister's words. She was thinking about her husband and how he would not be present at their child's birth. He would have made a wonderful father. When young children were around, he would steal a few minutes to play with them, running slowly so their small legs could keep up with him. Then laughing, he would fall to the ground as though exhausted, and the children would stumble and fall around him. Other times, he would sit quietly with them and tell stories that would bring smiles to their young faces. All these memories brought tears to her eyes.

"He will always be with you." Ruth gently reminded, sensing her sister's sadness.

"I know," Mary answered softly as she wiped the wetness from her eyes.

They spent the rest of the morning planning for the baby's arrival. Before long, laughter could be heard coming from the kitchen as the two young women made a list of items they would need for the baby's care.

The morning of the next prayer meeting dawned bright and clear with the promise of a warm sunny day ahead. The sisters walked together to the hillside. Although she was anxious to hear her sister preach, Ruth also worried about Mary's safety. It had only been four months since her husband had been brutally murdered. And, Ruth feared the same angry crowds might stir up trouble for her sister, after all, she was the Rabbi's widow.

The gently rolling hillside where they were to meet was just on the outskirts of the city, easily accessible from all directions. The two women were the first to arrive, soon followed by a local merchant who delivered the bread and wine ordered for the celebration. Mary had decided to use a flat rock surface as her table, and covered it with a large white cloth she had brought from home.

Ruth could see the excitement on her sister's face as she stepped back to view the table she had set. Ruth knew Mary had spent much time contemplating the prayers, teachings, and words she would say in this celebration. This worship service would be celebrated as none had been before. She was now ready to lead her husband's followers.

As people settled on the grassy area waiting for the service to begin, Mary noticed some of her husband's disciples, James, John, and Andrew, were among those present, and she went to greet them. Each embraced her warmly, truly happy to see her.

"We heard you were going to have a baby, now we can see for ourselves it is true," said James excitedly, with John nodding in agreement.

"And, when he is older, your son can lead as his father did before him," commented Andrew, his voice full of fatherly advice.

"You have got him grown before he is even born," Mary quickly replied, a smile on her face showing Andrew she was not taking his words seriously.

"I understand, but if there is anything we can do, please let us know, Andrew replied.

"Of course. After all, I am counting on all of you to be part of my child's life. It will be good for him to have men of faith in his life, especially friends of his fathers."

Mary smiled at each of the men. Then turning she moved to the front of the gathered crowd, noticing there seemed to be more people in attendance than previously. With her presence before them, the crowd became quiet with anticipation. She welcomed them warmly in a strong voice. The joy on the people's faces as she spoke gave her the confidence to continue.

These people, who had once so deeply loved her husband, were now showing her that same love and respect. Overwhelmed by their love, she knew in her heart this was what she was meant to be doing with her life.

Mary started the service with a blessing for the people, and led them in an ancient song of thanksgiving. Across the hillside, the people raised their voices in song to their god, singing the ancient words of praise.

Prayers of worship followed the singing, including the prayer to the father her husband had taught them. At the end of the prayers, she talked about her husband's love for his people.

"Although he is gone from this earth, he is with us in spirit. We must continue to care for each other, and love one another as he has loved us." She repeated her husband's words and people nodded in agreement. The lesson continued as she moved among the crowd enabling all to hear her. After several stories to emphasize her opening statement, she made her way towards the table she had set earlier.

With the eager eyes of the people upon her, Mary reverently lifted the flatbread from the table. Holding it in front of her for all to see, giving thanks she blessed the bread and broke off a piece, saying, "This is his body, which has been given for you. Do this in memory of him." With those words, she placed the bread in her mouth.

Next, she took a cup filled with new wine. Lifting it high, she gave thanks and blessed it, saying, "take this cup and share it among you. It is his blood, which has been shed for you."

Then, with the help of other women in the crowd, she served both the bread and wine to those present. The people remained in silent prayer as they experienced this sacred time. When all had received the gifts, Mary again turned to the crowd and gave them a final blessing saying, "go in peace."

As the crowd broke up, small groups gathered to talk about what they had just experienced. Many came forth to where she was standing and thanked her for sharing her husband's words. She was deeply touched by their comments, and promised to again share the breaking of the bread, as some had begun to call it.

The three apostles Mary had earlier spoken to were standing off to one side witnessing the people's reactions to the prayer service. Their faces showed concern for what they had just witnessed. And once Mary was by herself they quickly took her aside with words of admonishment.

"Mary, what are you doing? How can you share with strangers what Jesus told us in an intimate gathering? You should not be doing this"

"You are wrong. He wanted his people to share in the same experience. Remember, he said, 'Do this in remembrance of me.' He wanted all of us present, you and me and the other apostles, to do exactly as he had done that evening," she emphatically told the three men.

"We agree, but it is not safe. There were people in the crowd who could make trouble for you. They could report you to the officials and have you arrested just as your husband was. Think of the child, Mary!"

She could see the concern on their faces. They truly believed she had been wrong in sharing the events of the last supper so soon.

"I think we need to have Peter's advise on this," said John. With strained goodbyes, the men left in search of their leader.

Mary felt sad that the men did not agree with her, but she knew she had done the right thing in sharing the mystery of the bread and wine. Since her husband's death, many of the apostles hid from public ministry in fear of their lives, their courage diminishing with the death of their spiritual leader. Mary on the other hand, had been spiritually uplifted by the new ritual. She was not fearful, as were her husband's friends, who now hurried from the hillside.

While she had been talking to the people, Ruth had been packing up the cup and plate, wrapping them in the tablecloth. Mary thanked her sister for her help, and Ruth complimented her. "It was a beautiful service, I am so glad I was present."

"Thank you. I only wish John and the others felt the same. I know we were meant to share the events of the meal and not keep them to ourselves."

Chapter 32

The sisters started to leave the hillside when an excited group of women approached them. Among them was a young woman carrying an ill child. They were asking Mary to help the young one, who had been sick for days.

"Please," cried the mother. "Please heal my baby. She is so sick, and I fear she does not have long to live. Help me," she cried again as she lifted the lifeless child toward Mary.

"I do not have the power to heal," Mary replied as the child was thrust into her arms. "I am sorry," she sorrowfully told the distraught mother, feeling the lifeless form in her arms.

"You are his wife. You are carrying his child. How can you not heal my child?" The anguished young woman cried. Though her tears fell, she had faith that Mary could perform miracles.

"We can pray," whispered Mary, not knowing what else to say. As she prayed, she held the child close and stroked the small face, calling on god to save the infant. Feeling helpless, Mary's tears soon joined those of the others around her. Her tears gently splashed onto the tiny body in her arms.

Suddenly the infant began crying loudly and squirming where before she had been lifeless. Not knowing what to do, Mary quickly handed the child back to her mother. Safely in her mother's arms, the crying ceased. The baby was now breathing normally, and her cheeks had a pink glow of health.

Mary stood in awe as she was showered with thanks from the young mother and the others present. Upon returning home, she contemplated the day's events, realizing she had been given the gift of healing, which had once been her husband's. She fell to her knees, thanking the father.

Several days after the prayer service, Joseph came to Mary's house concerned for her safety. He had recently returned from a business trip and regretted not being present at the prayer service. He had heard of Mary healing the sick child. It was all over town, an official's wife had been present at the healing. And, now even the ruling authorities were talking about what had happened. This scared Joseph.

"There is much talk in the village and throughout the local towns about you performing a miracle. The officials are greatly concerned, and they have called a meeting to address what should be done about it. Mary, you must stop!" he exclaimed with concern. "You are in grave danger and would be at their mercy should you be called before them."

Mary took his words seriously and asked what she should do.

"I don't think it is safe to remain here. I know you had planned to raise the child in your family home, but I believe you should leave quickly and seek shelter in an area not under Roman rule."

"He's right," agreed Ruth. "After all, you also have the child to think of. Maybe you could go back to Egypt to live until things quiet down."

"Listen to your sister, Mary. It is not safe to remain here. Who knows what will happen at this meeting."

"But, how will I travel?" questioned Mary looking down at her belly with concern for the baby she carried. She did not question Joseph's motives; both had been present at her husband's trial and knew how quickly the crowds could be incited.

Mary trusted Joseph, knowing he spoke truthfully. He was a wealthy merchant with links into the political arena, both locally and in Rome.

"I have a large caravan of goods leaving early tomorrow for Alexandria. It would be easy to add another wagon comfortably outfitted for your travel, and I would go with you. This is my normal business routine, so no suspicion would be aroused. Late tonight we could move your belongings to my home. You would stay the night and be ready to leave with the caravan at dawn. This way, you would not be noticed leaving town. The trip is long, but I believe you would be safe, and settled long before the birth of your baby."

Mary heeded Joseph's words. With her sister's help, she managed to pack for the journey. It was a sad time for the sisters. They had grown close since her return and now would be separated for a long time. Joseph had promised to remain by her side. He would send for Ruth when he felt it was safe. Both women were saddened to know it would be a long time before they would see one another again.

Late that night, Mary made her way to Joseph's estate, taking a back road to avoid seeing anyone. Joseph, along with her brother and sister, had come to help move her belongings. Tearful goodbyes were said, along with promises to join her when it was safe to follow.

Chapter 33

Joan had downloaded the stolen manuscript to her computer. What she was reading was even more fascinating than she had hoped it would be. The description of the pendant and the meaning behind it was clear to Joan now. She had not let on that she knew anything about the pendant when Rachel had talked about it as proof. Yet, Joan was elated to think this may be the real pendant, which the Cardinal had referred to. It would be of great value historically, simply for the fact that it lent credibility to the so-called myth of Jesus and Mary as husband and wife. Joan's greedy mind could not even imagine the monetary value the pendant could have if offered to certain parties who would want it kept secret. Never mind that Rachel had something else that was proof of this ancient union that could be even more valuable. The pendant, and whatever else Rachel had would be Joan's secret for the time being. She needed to consider all her options to maximize her income from all angles before selling Rachel's book and promoting it to the top of the bestseller list. Joan was positive she could play both sides of the fence and come away with more wealth than she ever dreamed of having.

Clearly, she would need to do some strategic planning because timing would be key to her financial success. She decided now would be a good time to give Santini this part of the manuscript. That way the Council would be even more concerned about the book when they read about the gift of the pendant, which had long been rumored to exist. Joan would lay the groundwork by hinting to Santini that for the right price she might be able to present proof of the existence of a certain item in the story. She reached for the phone.

"Chaplain, this Joan Hale. I think we need to meet." She could imagine the petty little man starting to perspire nervously at the other end of the phone.

"Certainly Ms Hale. Do you have something for me?" Instantly he knew he sounded over anxious. He detested his lack of self-control, especially dealing with someone as sly as this woman.

In her most charming voice Joan replied, "why yes I do, but it is not free. I will require half of the balance owed for this very informative section." She waited patiently.

"I'll need to check with my superiors, but I think that's fair. Shall we meet tomorrow afternoon?" Santini wiped his brow.

"My office, two o'clock, and Michael, tell your superiors I can obtain something much more valuable to them than the manuscript, if the price is right." She clicked the receiver before he could respond.

Smiling, Joan put her glasses back on and continued to read the manuscript.

Chapter 34

In the darkness of the pre-dawn hours, while Mary slept, Joseph and his servants stocked the caravan wagon that would be her home for the long journey into Egypt. Besides the food and water that were crucial to their survival, he saw to it the wagon was outfitted with the finest bedding and cushions from his home. The journey would be long and hard, he was trying to make Mary's new surroundings as comfortable as possible.

At first light, Mary was awakened to the sound of a soft knock at her door. A house servant told her all was ready for her departure and the morning meal would be served shortly. Slipping from the warm bed, she sleepily made her way toward a burning oil lamp, raising the flame to light the dark room. Then she walked over to the washing table with its waiting water pitcher. She was tired, her body ached from lack of sleep. The late night move from her family home had been physically exhausting, and the sad goodbyes emotionally draining. With much on her mind, sleep had not come easily, she had tossed and turned through much of the night. Now, with the early rising, she did not feel well.

She poured cool water from the pitcher, splashing it onto her face to open her eyes, still heavy with sleep. She continued with a sponge bath, enjoying the luxury that would not be hers again until she reached her final destination. Choosing to wear simple loose clothing, layered for warmth, she was grateful she had taken Ruth's earlier advice to have larger clothing made.

When she was ready, she extinguished the lamp. Approaching the kitchen, the aroma of sweet breads, and other foods made her realize she was hungry. Joseph greeted her as she entered the room, accompanying her to the waiting foods.

"Eat heartily," he said. "On the road, our foods will be simple, so enjoy."

As she filled her plate with the wonderful selection of foods, he told her his news.

"I have a surprise for you. With the birth of your baby not too far off, I felt it might be wise for you to have a companion for the journey. I have asked your friend, Ashera to attend you, and she has agreed. She is outside now seeing to the details.

Mary was touched by his thoughtfulness and quickly finished her breakfast, so she might greet her friend. The wagon was nearly ready. She found her friend giving last minute orders about the placement of her belongings. The two hugged, Mary thanked Ashera for joining her. The sun was just coming over the horizon as they helped Mary into the waiting wagon, with Joseph giving her last minute details about the journey.

"The other wagons are waiting outside the estate walls. We will ride in the middle, I have taken this journey many times, the caravan should not be suspect for any reason. I will ride up front with your driver, Ahmed, who is a long time trusted worker. The wagons are heavy with goods, and the drive will be slow and tedious. Keep the coverings over the wagon openings, at least until we are several days journey from here. Besides hiding you from passersby, they will also help keep the dust from your quarters."

His instructions were short and to the point, with every precaution taken to ensure her safety. This was a side of Joseph she had never seen. With his attention to detail, Mary knew she was in good hands and felt confident about the journey.

Hidden in the caravan, as it moved through the village, Mary recognized voices of townspeople. She hated leaving them in secrecy and felt a deep sadness. Had it not been for the child she was carrying, she would have stayed, taking her chances with the local officials. Yet, she needed to protect her child, and had no choice, but to flee.

The first day's journey, like the many to follow, was hot and dusty, with the wagon bumping along each stone and rut in the road. The wagon, that had looked so comfortable at the onset of the journey, now jolted the women with each turn of the wheel. It wasn't long before Mary's body was stiff and sore from the constant battering. Even sitting had become uncomfortable for her with her large belly resting on her outstretched legs.

"It might be easier if you were lying down," suggested Ashera as she helped her adjust to a new position. Ashera had been sitting cross-legged on a large pillow, fairly comfortable leaning against the wagon wall.

Her friend, on the other hand, found little comfort outstretched on the bedding.

They passed the time reminiscing, recalling past times when both had regularly traveled back and forth to the temple in Alexandria. Although they had also traveled in a wagon then, there had been opportunities to walk and stretch their cramped legs, while talking and laughing with the other young women in their party. When their legs became tired, they would climb back into the luxury of the wagon for rest.

Now, Mary did not have such options. Before long, the wagon walls began to feel more like prison walls, restricting every movement. With the constant jarring from the rough terrain, she would frequently have to use the provided chamber pot. At first embarrassed, both women eventually adjusted to their primitive accommodations.

Late each afternoon, with the coming of sunset, the wagons halted in a clearing, forming a circle for protection. The simple evening meal was cooked over an open fire and served hot to the hungry men. With Ahmed, standing outside the wagon as guard, Joseph dined with the women, discussing the day's travel. The evening visit became the high point of each long day, with Mary's respect and gratitude growing for this man who had been her husband's friend.

Shortly after the evening meal, with nightfall, the camp would settle down to sleep. Since it was not safe on the open road after dark, the men took turns keeping watch through the night for any signs of robbers or warring tribes. Since Joseph's caravans traveled these roads often, he was well known to the local tribal leaders and usually passed in safety. However, he took no chances with his precious cargo and always posted guards.

The first few nights, Mary found it difficult to fall asleep. Lack of exercise and the cold desert nights kept her awake, her tired body screamed for rest. In the dark hours of early morning, she would finally drift off to sleep, only to be awakened several hours later by the noise of the rising workers. A hot morning meal was eaten in haste, with the men eager to resume their travel.

Day after day, the ritual was the same, as the wagons rolled on towards the Egyptian port of Alexandria. Each tedious mile brought Mary closer to her new home and the safety it provided from those who were a threat to her in Galilee. As the days progressed and Joseph became more assured of Mary's safety, he would briefly allow her the freedom and luxury of exercising. She reveled in being able to stretch her aching body by walking alongside the wagon.

But, as the days drew on, she found walking to be more difficult. The slow moving wagons were moving faster than she could now walk. She would be relieved when the child was born.

Chapter 35

One bright sunny morning as the men were readying to break camp, Mary and Ashera were outside their wagon enjoying the cool fresh air. Both women breathed deeply as they walked in circles stretching their legs before re-entering their wagon for the day's journey.

Suddenly, out of nowhere, the wind came up and the sand beneath their feet rose up in swirling dust. It quickly became painful, pelting their bodies as they hurried to take shelter in their wagon. As Ashera helped Mary into the wagon, Joseph came running towards them.

"Stay inside and cover yourselves," he screamed above the deafening wind. "A sand storm is moving in fast."

As he ran from wagon to wagon shouting orders, workmen could be seen quickly tying down loose items. Ashera settled Mary on her bedding and quickly closed the heavy cloth over the opening of their wagon. Fine dust was settling everywhere, and only the sound of the screeching wind could be heard.

Mary was sitting on the padded wagon floor with several blankets draped around her, ready to tent herself and Ashera in the protective covering. Words were of no use with the deafening sounds that engulfed them, so she motioned with her hand for Ashera to join her. As both women huddled under the darkness of the covers, the wind shook the wagon with fury. Both women feared the wagon would blow over. Even under several layers of cloth, the fine dust found its way to the women's faces. Their nostrils burned as they breathed the dusty air, and their eyes stung even though they kept them closed.

It seemed like an eternity before the wind died down. Eventually the blowing sand retreated back to the earth, and the world about them became silent. The women slowly shed the covering blankets, but the air was still thick with dust particles. Sand was everywhere inside the wagon, and they were stunned with what they saw. As Ashera helped Mary up, Joseph threw back the outside tarp, checking to see that both were unharmed.

"One wagon has been torn apart by the wind, and the driver was killed," he told them anxiously. "So we are going to stay here another night. It will give us time to gather what we can and check the safety of the other wagons. I'll be back again later." He left to assess the rest of the damage.

As Mary and Ashera stepped from their wagon, they pulled their shawls over their heads and across their faces to shield themselves from the settling dusty air. Filtered by rays from a hidden sun, the daylight had an eerie look about it. The women could barely see items scattered all around them. The wagon Joseph had spoken about was a heap of wood on the horizon.

While the men set about their work, the women returned to their wagon to give it a thorough cleaning. Ashera did the heavy work of shaking sand from bedding and blankets while Mary swept the wagon floor. They worked energetically with gratitude in their hearts for having come through the storm alive.

That day the sun had a second dawning, as the dust settled and the blue sky once again became visible. With their home in order and cleaned as best it could be, they went out into the warm sun to rest. Mary leaned against the wagon for support. She was tired. They had been traveling for many days and during that time she slept little. Her whole body ached from the rough travel and the extra weight of the baby.

Mary looked at her friend standing nearby. "You are covered with dust, Ashera. You look like a ghost." She laughed.

"You are no beauty yourself." She pushed Mary's curls back to view her gray face.

Both woman burst into laughter as they eyed each other head to toe. Laughter was such a relief from the tension of the morning's danger. Afterwards, they set about cleansing themselves of their ghostly looks.

The afternoon passed with Mary taking short walks, enjoying the freedom from the four walls of the wagon. The warmth of sun made her smile as she turned her face up towards the bright light. She thought about the journey so far. Until that morning, one day had blended into another with mundane routines. She had faired well, even with the lack of sleep, but could not help wondering if she had made this journey needlessly. She sighed with the realization she had to trust Joseph's wisdom in this move. Clearly, he was only trying to keep her and the baby safe from the same possible fate as her husband. Mary shuddered, quickly turning her thoughts to more pleasant memories.

Lost in thought, she did not see Joseph running towards her and was startled when he grabbed her arm.

"Quick, get back into the wagon," he commanded breathlessly. "There is an army of soldiers approaching and you should not be seen." He quickly helped her into the wagon. "Where's Ashera?"

"I don't know," Mary stammered with a fearful look on her face.

"I will find her, but no matter what happens, stay hidden until I come to you."

Joseph jumped from the wagon and went looking for Ashera. However, his search had to be abandoned quickly as soldiers thundered into camp on horseback.

Though covered with dust from the earlier storm, the red cloaks of the feared Roman soldiers were still recognizable. They were a common sight on the well-traveled road, and normally their passing would not be a concern. Joseph breathed deeply to quiet his thumping heart, attempting to appear calm. Greetings were exchanged as the Captain dismounted from his horse.

"We were caught without shelter in this morning's storm and lost most of our supplies and water. Could you spare us enough provisions to continue our journey? We can pay you for your generosity."

Joseph informed the soldier he too had lost supplies, but would see what could be spared. He really did not want to part with any of his supplies, but neither did he want to see the soldiers stay around any longer than necessary. With the help of several of his men, supplies were packed and handed over to the Captain. Joseph declined payment, wishing the men well on their journey.

It was not until they were well out of sight that he went to check on Mary. Folding back the wagon covering, he stepped inside. Finding her quietly huddled alongside a stack of pillows and blankets, he helped her up, holding her to quiet her shaking body.

"They are gone," he assured her. "They only wanted to replace the food and water they lost in the morning storm, but we could not take any chances."

"I know," whispered Mary as she came to the realization she did not want to live her life in fear.

Moments later, Ashera entered the wagon with Mary exclaiming, "Where have you been? I have been so worried about you."

"I'm sorry. Like you, I had been out walking. When I saw the soldiers approaching the camp, I knew I could not get back here without being noticed, so I quickly hid in another wagon until I heard the horses ride away."

The two women were left to exchange stories. Joseph hurried back to the work of readying his wagons for the next day's journey. Although time had been lost, most of the scattered cargo had been recovered, leaving him with few material losses, but devastated by the loss of one of his men. Yet, he was grateful for everyone else's safety, especially that of Mary and her child.

Chapter 36

Rachel sat in a private room at the bank, the safe deposit box before her. It had been many years since it had been opened. She donned a pair of white cotton gloves from her purse, well aware that handling rare books and papers could damage them. She would be extra cautious handling this priceless artifact. Lifting the lid of the box, her hands were shaking with anticipation, so she rested them on the velvet pad laid out in front of her. Slowly taking a couple deep calming breaths, she considered the enormous effect the disclosure of this one document could have on the world.

Mariah sat in the rocking chair in her baby's nursery. She was pleased with the way the room had turned out. She rubbed her hands over the arms of the chair. Grand had surprised her with the gift of this rocking chair. She told Mariah she had used it when Mariah's mother was an infant. As with the four-poster bed, it made Mariah feel closer to her mother. With the imminent birth of her baby, she had been thinking about her mother and missing her very much.

John called that afternoon to tell her Peter had been transferred to a psychiatric institution. He had been determined incompetent to stand trial and would be locked up in this hospital indefinitely. The doctors were not optimistic about him recovering. They felt he was probably an unstable person long before he went to Iraq, but the horrors he had witnessed there pushed him over the edge. His severe mental illness now made it unlikely he would ever return to reality. Mariah was relieved, yet felt a twinge of sadness for Peter. Like her husband, Joe, Peter was unmistakably another tragic statistic of this awful war.

Rachel gently lifted the scarlet cloth covered roll out of the box and set it on the velvet pad, carefully removing the cloth. Sighing, with her hands shaking again, she hesitated for a moment. She picked up the disposable camera she had brought and clicked a couple pictures of the scroll from different angles. She untied the purple ribbon, which held it closed. Then ever so gently unrolled it and held it flat with her gloved hands. Her heart was pounding, as she looked over the ancient prophecy once again. Carefully weighting it down at each end, she took several pictures of the document. Then lifting another piece of paper from the box and unfolding it carefully she began to read the translation of the ancient prophecy, even though she knew it well. She mouthed the words, *"... and when the first born of the first born is ... "* Rachel stopped, giving serious thought to this yet to be fulfilled prophecy. She considered Mariah, and then thought anything is possible. Carefully she placed the precious papers back in the bank box, having no intention of offering Joan the translation. The fact that the scroll was ancient would have to suffice.

Rachel had decided she could not risk anything happening to this precious document. Pictures of it would be adequate evidence, for the time being. Her manuscript was the untold true story of Mary Magdalene, and the scroll was the legitimate supporting proof. She did not trust Joan, so the pictures were a safer form of proof, while still protecting the treasure. Removing her pendant, she also took a few pictures of it to include in her book, as tangible proof for the readers.

Joan's calls were weekly since they made their deal. It was so much better for Rachel that she actually did not mind talking to her now. She was at her computer when the phone rang.

"Hello, darling, how are you? How's it going?" Joan asked all in one breath.

"Hello, Joan. I am well and you?" Rachel paused politely.

"Fine, fine. I am anxious to hear how my favorite author is progressing."

Rachel laughed. "Well, the book is coming along nicely. I am very pleased with my latest chapters, and I've had a new idea."

"Really, tell me!" Joan said excitedly.

"Well, I thought about the proof that my family legend is true. I have decided to include pictures of my pendant in the book, as evidence for the readers."

"Smashing, Rachel, what an excellent idea!" Joan hesitated choosing her words carefully. "Did you think about sharing this other proof you mentioned you have?"

"Yes, Joan. I have taken pictures of my other proof. I decided the item is too fragile and precious to be handled by others. I think the pictures will be sufficient evidence, at least for now." She expected an argument, so was surprised by the agent's reaction.

"Great, I will trust your judgment, I'm sure you know what's best in this situation. When can I see the pictures?"

"I'll let you know as soon as I get them developed, and we'll set up a date. Oh, and I am sorry to make you come here again, but I don't want to go too far with Mariah so close to delivery."

"Not a problem, Hon. Just let me know when." Joan could barely contain her excitement until she got off the phone. She thought for only a minute and immediately started dialing Santini's number.

Chapter 37

The first major snow storm of the season hit on a weekend. Mariah woke up early on Saturday morning. She was so uncomfortable lying down it wasn't worth trying to go back to sleep. She rolled to a sitting position and moaned, her back had been aching for a few days now. She made her way slowly downstairs.

Grand was in her study and called good morning to her saying, "Get your tea and bring it in here by the fire." A few minutes later Mariah lumbered into the study and tried to make herself comfortable on the loveseat by the fireplace. Rachel was seated at her desk.

"How are you feeling, sweetie?"

"Not great, grand. My back has been really bothering me, and I have a hard time sleeping because I am so uncomfortable." Mariah took a sip of her tea, gazing out the window at the winter wonderland behind her grandmother.

"Well, Hon cheer up. You don't have long to go!"

"Yes, I know. Did you see how much snow there is out there?" Rachel nodded. "Grand let's decorate for Christmas today!" Mariah sounded like an excited child.

"That's a wonderful idea. Maybe we could bribe John to pick up a Christmas tree by inviting him to dinner." They both laughed knowing John would do anything for a home cooked meal. The phone rang right then, and Rachel answered it.

"Good morning Rachel, my dear. How are you?" asked James kindly.

"Why, James, I was just thinking of you. Would you like to come to dinner this evening and help us decorate the Christmas tree?"

"Rach, I couldn't think of anything I would enjoy more on a beautiful winter day like today. I'll pick up some wine and dessert."

"Wonderful, James. Come early, say five o'clock?" She was so animated whenever she was around James, or even talking to him, it was apparent to Mariah how she felt about him.

Rachel had a broad smile on her face, which told Mariah Dr. James had agreed. She knew he was special to Grand, but could never understand over the years why the relationship had not gone further.

Hesitantly Mariah asked, "Grand, I have a personal question I've wanted to ask you for a long time."

"My dear, you can ask me anything. You should know that by now."

"I know it's not my business, but you and James have been so close, for so long. Why haven't you ever married or moved in together?" Mariah looked at the fireplace a little embarrassed to being prying into her grandmother's personal life.

Rachel appeared quite serious. "Honey, we did consider both over the years, but for one reason or another the timing just never seemed to be right. Who knows it might still happen one of these days." She gave her granddaughter a wink and pushed the phone towards her. "Now you call your very good friend."

Mariah blushed. "Oh Grand, he is just a friend."

"The best relationships start out that way, my dear! Now call him," Grand ordered smiling, as she rose to leave the room.

They spent much of the day decorating the inside of the house. It was really taking on a festive air. John arrived first with a beautiful full tree that he immediately set up in the living room so the branches would have time to come down before they decorated it. In the meantime, James arrived with two huge brilliant red poinsettias he placed on either side of the fireplace in the living room. He then brought in two more, which were white with gold ribbons streaming from their centers. He put these in Rachel's study on the sides of that fireplace. He walked by Rachel, kissing her on the cheek as he went out to his car again. Rachel laughed, he was very sweet, and even at her age he made her heart beat a little quicker when he was close.

John and Mariah were sitting in the living room slowly taking out the tree decorations, as she told him the history behind each one. James poured three glasses of wine and a cranberry juice for Mariah. The house seemed to be filled with happiness for the first time since Joe's death. James made a toast. They all held their glasses up.

"Here's to a wonderful holiday season and a future filled with happiness for all of us." The four glasses clinked, but his eyes were lovingly fixed on Rachel.

The conversation was lively all through dinner with everyone sharing stories of past holidays. It seemed there was no end to the laughter and playfulness of the evening. It felt magical as they decorated the Christmas tree. Rachel played holiday music softly in the background, at times they even sang along. As they transformed the evergreen into a sparkling wondrous symbol of the Christmas season, a feeling of renewal and hope enveloped them. When they were finished they all stood back in silence, marveling at the beauty they had created. John now raised his glass.

"I would like to make a toast too." They all picked up their glasses.

"Here's to the holiday season. May it bring new love and peace to the whole world!" The sound of glasses clinking together echoed through the house, as did his words.

Chapter 38

Michael Santini nervously awaited Cardinal Leary. As he sat in the New York Cardinal's opulent office, he felt his courage waning. He was no longer so confident his intended proposal would produce the rewarding result he hoped for, or if it would be the end of his lousy career. He took out his hanky, mopped his brow, and thought I must not appear nervous. This was his one shot at being more than a Chaplain for the rest of his life. If it worked it would be his ultimate dream come true. His lifelong yearning for power would finally be fulfilled.

The Cardinal entered his office with his usual regal air of authority, instantly intimidating Santini.

"What is it I can do for you Michael?" There was no pleasant greeting or pretense of welcome.

The Chaplain knew Cardinal Leary was aggravated with him for daring to come to his office in person. "Well, Cardinal Leary I have an interesting proposition for the Council, and felt it was best explained to you in person."

The Cardinal eyed the agitated little man doubtfully. Wondering what he could possibly have, which would be of the slightest interest to the Council.

"Alright Michael, continue."

"It's about the legend, the manuscript. The agent I've been dealing with has more of it. I have a meeting tomorrow to buy it from her, if you approve the money transfer." He waited, starting to perspire now.

"That will be fine, but what are you proposing to the Council?" The Cardinal was growing impatient.

"I can obtain information more valuable than the manuscript. It is something, which will prove the legend is true. Something, which I am quite sure the Council would not want made public!" Santini was so excited he had to use his hanky to wipe his upper lip.

The Cardinal was not saying anything. He seemed to be deep in thought, slowly tapping his fingers on the desk, while staring out the window. Finally he looked at the chaplain.

"What exactly is it, Michael, you would want for this information?" Thomas Leary's face had gotten quite dark, his voice had an edge of danger, and his look was threatening.

Santini shifted in his chair, trying to sit taller to boost his courage. "In trade for this priceless information I would require a seat on the Council." He sat steadfast with his gaze boldly fixed on the Cardinal, expecting a clap of thunder with the response.

Again, Cardinal Leary stared blankly out the window, but for a longer time. He slowly turned his chair towards Santini.

"Michael this is a serious, if not foolish deal you propose. I will not present this to the Council until I have more substantial proof that what you are offering is valid information." He sighed and leaned back in his chair.

"Of course, Cardinal, I understand. I will have that proof for you as soon as possible." Santini stammered slightly, "But obviously I will have to know I have deal with the Council before I give full disclosure of the information."

Thomas Leary was not a patient man on his best day, and he did not like Michael Santini to begin with. He was having a difficult time restraining his temper. The audacity of this conniving little man enraged him. Who did he think he was to make deals with The Council of Religion? He was way out of his league, and too ignorant to even know it.

"Yes, well you work it out however you can. I am simply telling you I will not embarrass myself by addressing the Council with trivial information." With that comment, the Cardinal stood, signaling the meeting was over.

Chapter 39

Rachel laid out the pictures on her desk in an effort to pick the best ones to give to Joan. She figured two of each view of the scroll and two pictures; front and back, of the pendant should be sufficient proof for Joan. Her agent would be arriving that evening, and she did not want her choosing the pictures.

Joan sat in Rachel's study fascinated by the photographs before her. She had already believed the pictures of the pendant were valuable, but this ancient scroll was a whole different ball game.

"Do you know what it says?" Joan asked, eyes affixed on the pictures.

"Of course I do, Joan, but that is not something I am comfortable disclosing, not at this time anyway," Rachel replied firmly.

"Okay. We'll simply stash the pictures of the scroll away in case we need to come up with more proof to back the validity of your book. Do you still want to use the pendant pictures in the book?"

"I believe it would be a good idea. I feel it lends historic credibility to the whole story."

"I agree," Joan replied still looking at the pictures. "Will you be finished soon?"

"I can confidently say I will be finished the book before Christmas. Actually, I have more for you right now," Rachel responded proudly, handing her a folder with her latest material in it. "I only have a couple chapters to go."

"That's fabulous! I am looking forward to reading the whole story. And also getting a bidding war going with the publishers!" Joan winked at her, as she put her coat on to leave. "Merry Christmas, Rachel, give Mariah my best, and let me know when the new baby arrives."

Back in her office the next day Joan surveyed the pictures. She carefully placed the ones of the scroll in an envelope and locked them in her safe. She then clipped the pendant pictures to the folder marked with Rachel's name and placed the folder in her desk draw.

She had figured out her strategy for maximizing her return on all the information she had obtained from Rachel. She dialed Santini's number. Joan explained to him she had photographs of an ancient item, which backed the legend. And she would be willing to share these, for a price separate from that of the manuscript.

She intended to sell him the scroll pictures, while keeping the existence of the pendant a secret until the book was published. She would make a fortune. She would deceive the Council into thinking they had silenced the proof, by purchasing the scroll pictures. And, she wouldn't really be breaking her deal with them by publishing the other pictures with the book. It was just a slight omission of information, which consequently would net her a hefty profit.

Chapter 40

Santini sat in his office, with its tacky Christmas decorations of tinsel and blinking lights, considering his phone conversation with Joan Hale. He was thinking about what his next move should be. He weighed his options. He could over charge the Cardinal, under pay Joan, making a pretty penny, and still demand a seat on the Council for getting the information. But then, they may not give him the position, if they had to buy the information from Joan. He was picking his teeth with a toothpick when a sinister grin spread uncontrollably across his stubble covered face. He knew what he would do to get what he wanted.

He slipped by the front desk, which was fortunately empty at the moment, as was the lobby. The night watchman must have been in the men's room or something, or hopefully, he was just not very good at his job. Santini hurried to the already open elevator door, quickly closed the door, and pushed the button for Joan's floor. He cautiously stepped out of the elevator, looking down the hallway in both directions, all clear he thought. Hesitating momentarily, he wiped the perspiration from his dripping forehead and unbuttoned his heavy winter coat. He tried to walk quietly down the hall, but his wet boots made an echoing squeak with each step. It felt like all of New York could hear him. Santini stood in front of Joan's office door, working on the lock, for what seemed like an eternity, drops of sweat running down his nose and hitting the floor. Finally, the door opened. He prayed the inner door to her office would not be locked; it opened easily, another lucky break. Closing the door behind him, he turned on a light. He went directly to her file cabinets, but they were locked. There would probably be a key in her desk, so he pulled draws open, frantically looking for a key. There in the lower draw was a folder, with pictures clipped to it and Rachel's name on it. He only glimpsed at the photos. It was some kind of antique jewelry; it must be the proof Joan had referred to, there were additional chapters to the manuscript in the folder, also. Santini closed the draw, slipping the folder into the front of his coat. He was surprised at how easy this was, Joan should have been more cautious. Quietly opening the door to the outer office, he was surprised to be looking at a gun aimed directly at his chest.

"Hold it right there, buddy." ordered the security guard. Santini was so taken aback by the gun, he threw his hands in the air, the folder fell from his coat, it's contents scattering on the floor.

He started begging for the guard not to shoot. Michael Santini was so terrified he wet his pants, before the second guard even had the handcuffs on him. He had not considered the consequences of getting caught.

Joan received the phone call someone had broken into her office, but had been apprehended. The police needed her to come to her office to see if anything was missing. They said the man was caught with a folder of papers and some pictures. Joan knew instantly who the thief must be. *Santini, that stupid little sweaty creep! He'll ruin everything!*

Joan did not press charges, for her own sake. Anyway, Santini was handed over to the military authorities and relieved of his duties as Chaplain, pending a hearing to determine if he would be dishonorably discharged for his illicit actions.

Joan decided to take matters into her own hands, no more of this third party negotiating, no more pretending.

She would go directly to the power, one step away from the hierarchy of the whole deal. It could be dangerous to let on she knew who they were, but she would be able to clearly state her demands.

Cardinal Leary's assistant put Joan on hold for a few minutes, finally the Cardinal picked up.

"Good afternoon, Joan, How are you?" He asked quite causally.

"Why, Cardinal, actually this is one of the best days I have had in a long time. And I also expect it to be one of my most profitable." Joan was equally nonchalant.

She could feel the tension through the phone line. His tone became much sterner as he asked what he could do for her.

"No more games, Thomas. We both know Santini is out of the picture. I have some especially valuable proof that the legend is true, and if your superiors are willing to meet my price I'll throw in the last chapters of the book too."

"You are quite the business woman, Joan. Tell me what you require, and I'll see what I can do for you."

"I think you have that backwards, Cardinal. It's what I can do for the Council." She told him the price and without waiting for a response hung the phone up. It was quite apparent she held all the cards. Joan sat back in her chair, admiring the New York City skyline, and feeling particularly self-satisfied with her business savvy.

Chapter 41

The journey towards Egypt continued onward with one day blending into another. The daily routine was always the same, and the two women were becoming bored with each other. With nothing happening in their daily lives, they were running out of things to talk about to pass the time in their wagon. Mary was still not sleeping well at night and visible signs of the weariness were beginning to show on her face, around her eyes. She was increasingly irritable. Her body was taking a beating daily from the rough wagon ride, and the growing baby kept her awake much of the time kicking her. Mary had not been prepared for either, and she complained without considering how grateful she should be. After all, she and her baby were healthy, and they were safely enroute to Egypt, thanks to Joseph's help. She knew in her heart she could not have done this without trusting in his plan.

"I'm sorry, Ashera. I know I have complained much, but I just want this journey to end soon."

"I know. When we used to travel this way, it never seemed to take as long as this."

"Well, for one thing, I was not carrying a child, and these heavy supply wagons are much slower than the wagon we used to travel in."

"And, with the other young women traveling with us, we always had lots of laughter and stories to pass the time," replied Ashera to her friend.

One evening at supper, Joseph told the women they were close to the Egyptian border and would cross over in about a day or two, if all went well. His words brought joy to the two women.

"More than half of our journey is over," explained Joseph. "And, I have some news I think you will like. About a day's journey inside Egypt, just outside the town of Bersabee, we will come to the home of my good friend Benthar and his family. There we will camp for a few days, giving you some rest. I have sent one of the men ahead on horseback to inform him of our arrival.

The women were delighted with Joseph's news and listened eagerly as he continued, "After a day's rest, I will continue South with two of the wagons and head for the town of Elusa. After finishing my business there, I will return to you and we will continue on towards the coast. In my absence you will be safe, and I know you will enjoy the company."

The idea of spending several days off the road delighted Mary and Ashera, and the welcomed news lifted their spirits. On the day of their expected arrival, they were as anxious as two little children, wondering what their roadside home would be like. When their caravan pulled off the trade road, the two women were surprised to find a large estate, settled in a green oasis alongside a river.

In the doorway stood a large bearded man waving and shouting welcome. Mary could hear Joseph's voice in reply. When the wagons stopped, Joseph helped Mary and Ashera from the wagon just as his friend arrived at the wagon opening.

"Welcome, welcome, my friend," boomed Benthar in a loud voice rippled with laughter. The two men hugged and Benthar kissed Joseph on each cheek.

Joseph introduced the women to his friend and then they were quickly ushered into the kitchen to meet Benthar's wife. Nephra was a slim woman with dark hair knotted high on her head. Her softly lined face, weathered by the sun, featured large brown eyes lined with black kohl. It was a regal appearance often seen on wealthy Egyptian women. Her smile was warm and welcoming, and Mary quickly felt a kinship with this gentle woman.

Nephra showed Mary and Ashera to separate sleeping quarters that were elaborately and comfortably decorated. Next she showed them the bathing pool in a sheltered courtyard not far from their rooms. The water was clear and ran into the pool from a nearby cascading fall, creating a haven from their dust-filled journey.

"You have plenty of time before the sunset meal to bath and rest," informed Nephra. "And, I will send in a plate of fresh fruit for you to enjoy." The two friends excitedly thanked their hostess with plans to quickly return to the bathing area.

Mary was first to enter the beautifully tiled courtyard, and immediately she noticed a young servant girl placing a large plate of fresh figs and grapes on a low marble stand near the pool's edge. As she approached the steps, the servant extended her arms to catch the robe Mary shed as she entered the sun-warmed waters. Step by step, she descended into the tepid water inching her way forward, until her belly was nearly covered beneath the refreshing liquid. Then, Mary inched downward, allowing the water to totally cover her from head to toe. Never had she so appreciated the luxury of a bath as she did at that moment.

As her head re-emerged into the golden sunlight, Mary was startled by a big splash made by Ashera as she dove into the water. When Ashera came up for breath, Mary quickly splashed her friend in the face. Both women laughed, and each continued the childish water game for a few minutes. Then they made their way over to the waterfall where small jars of soap and scented oils sat on the pool's edge. The women quickly soaped their hair and bodies, breathing deeply of the clean fragrance. It took several latherings of the soap for the women to feel cleansed of their layers of dust and until their hair was again shiny. Then they took turns combing the scented hair oils into their tangled tresses.

Lingering at the pool's edge, nibbling on the provided fruit and talking, they enjoyed the sun on their wet bodies. "I could stay here forever," commented Mary, swirling the waters with her arms.

"I don't think so," laughed Ashera, "We are already beginning to look like dried fruit." Ashera held up her hands to reveal rippled skin and Mary laughed.

The cool waters had not only cleansed their skin, but had renewed conversation and camaraderie between the women. Where they once had grown silent in the wagon, now words and laughter flowed as freely as the water falling into the pool. As they climbed the stairs out of the water, the servant girl held open a fresh robe for each of the women to slip into. Ashera had decided to stay and lounge on a nearby chaise, enjoying the fresh outdoor air, while Mary returned to her room to nap before the evening meal.

Chapter 42

Upon awakening, Mary felt rested and refreshed, something she had not felt since leaving home. The bed had been soft and she had easily nestled into it, falling quickly asleep. Slowly she left the comfort of her bed, placing her feet onto a colorful soft rug, which nearly filled the entire floor space.

Barefoot she made her way to the window area, enjoying the soft fibers under her feet and between her toes. When the beautiful crimson draperies were parted, a lovely landscape of brightly colored flowers and tall shade trees were revealed, against the backdrop of a brilliant setting sun. Everything truly delighted Mary's senses, creating a feeling of happiness and security in this stranger's home.

Earlier in the day, Mary's travel bags had been carefully unpacked by a servant. Care had been taken to lie out her accessories, and several robes, once wrinkled, now ready to wear. Mary chose one of her new robes to wear to dinner and quickly changed into the blue silky fabric. Next, she swept her still damp curls onto the top of her head, winding her strand of pearls into the hair, and anchoring them with a small shell comb. She felt beautiful, and she smiled as her hand slowly moved along her belly, whispering to the child within, "Soon you will be in my arms, and you will be loved as I have loved your father."

She left her room and headed for the main part of the house that echoed with voices and laughter. Nephra was the first to greet her as she entered the room.

"You look lovely, Mary. I assume you rested well?"

"I did, and thank you for attending to our needs. You are most gracious." She noticed Ashera was already deep in conversation with a beautiful young women elegantly dressed.

Nephra linked her arm into Mary's and gently guided her to the center of the room where two other young women were happily talking with Joseph.

"I would like you to meet our daughters, Shemara, Rena, and Deborah." Each of the girls turned towards their mother at the mention of their names and introductions were made.

The oldest, Shemara, came forward first and warmly greeted Mary with a hug, followed by Rena and Deborah. Like their mother, the daughters had an exotic aristocratic look.

"Shemara is married and lives here with her husband, Ben, who runs our family business. Unfortunately, he is away at the moment, but we are happy Shemara does not have to be alone."

Mary envied Shemara as she sadly remembered the family she had to leave behind.

"Deborah is our youngest and spoiled by her father, but she is a great help to me in running the household. And, Rena is our traveler who is home for a short visit. She serves the goddess and lives at the temple in Alexandria. We are blessed by her presence."

"I too served at the temple," Mary quickly responded, looking at Rena who had been talking to Ashera.

"I remember you, Mary. You were the temple priestess when I first entered my training. I was excited when mother told me you were to be our guest for a few days."

"You will have plenty of time to visit," interrupted Nephra. "Now it is time to eat."

Everyone took a seat around a low circular table in the center of the room. Nephra fussed over Mary, making sure she was comfortable on her floor pillow, and Joseph smiled as he caught Mary's eye. Mary returned his smile, remembering how he had mentioned earlier she would enjoy this stay.

Voices subsided as each person hungrily ate from the delicious plates that were served. The rich combination of foods from this Egyptian region was a welcome change from the simple meals eaten on the road, and Mary savored every morsel. When the meal was finished, everyone lingered at the table, sipping on strong Egyptian coffee and talking.

"Mary," said Benthar as he leaned into the table to be closer to her, "I want you to know how sad I am at the death of your husband, and to say how welcome you are at our home."

"Thank you, Benthar. Your home has been such a respite from the long journey, I am truly grateful."

"I met your husband some time ago when I was on a business trip in your country. Joseph recognized my caravan and hailed me from a hillside where your husband was preaching. Since that time, I have heard much about his ministry, and of late, I have heard you are performing many of the same works as he."

"Yes, at first, my grief kept me from the followers. My husband had shared his ministry with me and without him by my side, I felt lost and alone. I missed him immensely, but as I sat among those who loved him and talked of his last days, I found my loneliness was lessened. As I became more confident at preaching his words, the crowds grew. Now the same people who killed my husband are angered by my works."

"Joseph and I had a long visit earlier today. He told me the details leading to your decision to leave Galilee for the safety of Alexandria. I understand that you need a safe place to raise your child, but I do not believe Alexandria will give you that safety. As Joseph knows, it is a busy port, but only those who live here realize how many Romans use it as a place of entry into this region. We have not been under Roman rule for many years, but there is still a large presence of soldiers and officials in this area, especially on the trade route you have been following. Many also linger in the city, resting after the journey across the sea. If word goes out for your capture, it won't be long before you are recognized."

Mary listened to Benthar, remembering how scared she had been when the soldiers entered their camp after the sandstorm. They had only wanted supplies, but they could easily have been looking for her.

"If I will not be safe in Alexandria, where shall I go?"

"I'm not sure. Joseph says you will give birth soon, so travel across the sea is out of the question. You would be welcome to stay here, but even here I cannot vouch for your safety. This area is busy with travelers from both our countries."

"Enough!" reprimanded Nephra, scowling at her husband. "You have scared us all. For now, Mary is safe and I am sure a solution will come before she has to leave us. Until then, we must make her days as pleasant as possible."

Nephra then led the ladies outdoors to enjoy the gardens, leaving the men to continue their talk. Gentle warm breezes and fragrant flowers soothed Mary's fears, and under starlit skies she silently prayed for her husband's help in finding a safe place to raise their child. The next morning Mary woke late, long after Joseph had left for Elusa, and she found Ashera helping Rena in the kitchen.

"Good morning," Rena greeted warmly. "We were just preparing you a plate of food."

"Mary, Rena thinks she has a plan for your safety in Alexandria," said Ashera excitedly.

Mary looked questioningly at Rena as she accepted the plate of food the young woman offered. "You have a plan to continue to Alexandria? Last evening your father said it would not be safe."

"Come, let us sit in the garden and while you eat, I will explain."

When the women were comfortably seated under a large sycamore tree, Rena began to speak. "Last evening we talked much about the goddess and how we all have served her people. Before bed, I prayed Isis would provide you safety and shelter for the birth of your child. I believe she has answered those prayers."

Mary was touched by the gentleness and caring of the woman before her. Although she was only slightly older than Mary, she displayed wisdom beyond her years.

"Isis is the creatress, giver of life. Her temple offers you sanctuary, Mary."

"How can she offer me sanctuary? I left her service, and I chose to worship the god of my husband."

"Don't you see, Mary? She is and always will be part of who you are, and she loves you still. She is the giver of life, the divine mother of us all. Just as her tree we sit under gives us shade, so shall her temple give you shelter. There you will be safe."

It had been a long time since Mary had thought of Isis and the many blessings she had in her power to bestow. Now, through Rena, Mary's own prayers had been answered, but she knew permission must first be granted by the high priestess.

"Mary, when I am in my mother's home, I am her child, and she introduces me as such. And although she told you I serve the goddess, she did not tell you it is I who serve Isis in the highest position as priestess," said Rena with great humility. "You do not need my permission, Mary, I offer you the sanctuary you need."

With tears in her eyes Mary gratefully hugged Rena as Ashera looked on. When the two separated, Rena raised her open arms towards the heavens and with palms open, she prayed aloud, "Isis, mother in the horizons of heaven … praise be unto thee, O lady, for the gifts you have given. Words of adoration rise unto thee from your humble servants."

Chapter 43

The morning of departure was hectic, even though the wagon had been packed the night before. Nephra insisted on adding additional bedding and blankets for the women's comfort, and baskets of fresh fruits and foods for their enjoyment. Good natured Joseph just kept rearranging things to accommodate the new items, and eventually the wagon was ready.

Rena had decided to shorten her family visit and travel with Mary and Ashera to Alexandria, ensuring easy entrance into the temple living quarters. Tearful goodbyes were said to Nephra and Benthar with gratitude for their hospitality.

"Take care of yourself, Mary, and may the goddess protect you and your baby," wished Nephra as she kissed her on the cheek.

"Thank you," whispered Mary with tears in her eyes. She and Ashera had been welcomed as family, and it was hard to say goodbye to this generous loving couple. As the wagons pulled away from the estate, Benthar and Nephra waved until the women were out of sight.

Inside the wagon, Ashera and Rena were busy rearranging bedding and pillows. The addition of a third person made for tighter quarters, but the women did not complain. As Mary watched her friends work, she silently gave thanks for their presence in her life.

Joseph had instructed the drivers to head East towards the coastal town of Raphia instead of taking the central more populated trade route along the Nile River. From Raphia, they would travel along the coast straight into the busy seaport of Alexandria, their destination.

The second half of the journey was more difficult for Mary. Each time she moved, she required help in the placement of cushions around her body for support and comfort against the jolting movement of the wheels. At the end of the day, when the wagons stopped, Ashera and Rena were needed to help Mary up from the floor, with Joseph assisting her off the wagon. Each night Mary took a walk by herself, gazing into the starlit skies above, watching the new moon grow little by little, knowing its fullness would be near the time of her baby's birth. Rena was a delightful addition to the traveling party. She had a way with words and gestures that created much laughter when she entertained them with her stories. Yet, one could see a deeper, more reflective side as she daily adhered to her prayerful devotions, waking early to honor the goddess in the rising sun. Midday she quietly prayed the prayers of petition, and before retiring, gave thanks for the day's blessings.

One day, Mary asked Rena if she would like to join Ashera and her in prayer, "After all, what strength our prayers would have as together they rise to the heavens."

"You would not be offended?"

"No, like the goddess, our god is benevolent, nurturing, and caring, and in our hearts we revere his presence in our midst just as you revere her. On this journey we have become like sisters, why not allow our joined prayer to continue to awaken the divine within us."

Henceforth, the bond between the three women grew and became strong as side-by-side they worshipped the divine presence in each of their lives. Rena often asked Mary to share her husband's teachings, realizing that his message of love, compassion, and helping others was similar to that of the goddess, wanting only what was best for their believers.

The closer they came to Alexandria, the more houses and camps became visible along the side the road. The city was over populated, and many people preferred living just outside the city limits in the open spaces.

Isis' temple was the largest building in Alexandria and could be seen long before they actually entered the city limits. The giant-sized white marble columns were impressive sitting atop the steps that led up to the temple entrance. As the wagons came nearer, Mary could see the two statues of Isis carved from each end pillar. The goddess stood tall and proud standing in her moon-boat. On top of her head she wore a crown with the all-seeing eye affixed in the center, the symbol of right, truth, and justice. The life-like figure gave the impression she was holding up the temple entrance, bidding her worshippers welcome.

The huge pillars never failed to impress Mary and the sight of them now invoked happy memories of earlier times spent serving the goddess.

"Rena, seeing the temple again, brings back wonderful memories, and I am so pleased you have offered me shelter here. Once again seeing the splendor of the temple entrance makes me feel as though I am coming home."

"You are not a stranger Mary, the temple will be your home for as long as you need it."

Joseph stopped just outside the gates to the temple, and helped Rena down from the back of the wagon. Once the colorfully dressed guards recognized her, they opened the gates wide for the wagon to pass. As the gates closed behind them, Rena led the wagon to a side entrance manned by guards. When the doors were opened, servants spilled out, welcoming the priestess, ready to do her bidding.

A stately woman with graying hair stepped forward to greet Rena, "Welcome home your highness. How may I help you?"

Quickly Rena explained about the guests she had brought with her, and as Joseph helped Mary out of the wagon, the woman gasped with delight, recognizing her from years past. The two quickly embraced and Mary smiled warmly at Shua. Rena escorted the tired women through the open doors, into a short corridor and up a flight of stairs into her large living chamber in the East wing of the Temple. The lavish quarters were spacious and reserved only for the priestess and her guests.

"Mary, it is fitting that you should stay in the upper chambers that were once your home. Come, make yourself comfortable, and Ashera, you will stay in the room next to hers." Ashera had never been in this part of the temple quarters, and her eyes were wide with excitement. Leaving them to settle in, Rena went to take care of temple business, promising to share the evening meal with her guests. Ashera took charge of Mary's belongings that were beginning to come up from the wagon, leaving Mary free to stroll onto a balcony that overlooked a beautiful private courtyard. The temple grounds were a haven from the dreariness of city life, and she appreciated the simple quiet.

It was late afternoon, and the reddish purple rays of the setting sun were streaming into Mary's room, letting her know that the evening meal was close at hand. She had bathed in the private pool in the courtyard below, and feeling refreshed, she dressed in one of her prettiest gowns, taking time to style her hair. Then, as had become habit, her hand automatically went to her throat. Caressing her pendant she always wore, she recalled her wedding day and how lovingly Jesus had placed the pendant around her neck. Momentarily saddened, she finished dressing with effort.

When the three women met in the dining area, they had a look of royalty about them, each standing tall and proud looking like goddesses.

"I trust your rooms are comfortable?" Rena graciously asked.

"They are as I remember them, spacious and beautiful. Thank You."

Ashera was awed by her luxurious surroundings and just nodded her assent to Rena. She could not believe her good fortune to be able to reside there. It was an experience that most temple women did not have, since the living quarters of the spiritual leader were private, affording her rest and quiet from other temple activities. This same privacy would also give Mary and her child the protection she sought from the eyes of the world about them.

In the days that followed, the women rested and settled into a routine. Shua, who had been asked to attend Mary and plan for the baby's birth, called in the temple physician. He confirmed the health of mother and child, and the expected birth to be near the time of the full moon.

In the pre-dawn hours of morning, on the eve of solstice, Mary awoke to a sharp pain that momentarily took her breath away. When she could, she called out to Ashera for help, which also awakened Rena. Soon the room was filled with the excitement of the impending birth, and none was happier than Mary that the process had begun.

Although it would be a while before the delivery, Rena gave orders to summon the midwife. Temple duties would keep her away until the next morning and she wanted to be sure Mary had everything she needed to be comfortable.

"Soon I will leave for the temple, and as you know, the services will last until sun up tomorrow. Until I return, Shua will see to your needs. You have only to ask."

"Thank You."

"May the great mother protect you and your child."

Rena then left for the solitude of the temple where she spent the day fasting and praying, preparing for the scared ritual that would start later that night.

The midwife set about preparing Mary's room, changing it from bedroom to birthing room, and placing a well-padded basket in the corner closest to Mary's bed where the child would sleep. Labor pains were sporadic throughout the day, giving Mary plenty of time to reflect on her new life as a mother, and she had some doubts. Sighing often and absently fingering her pendent, she stood quietly looking out over the gardens, wishing her husband were with her. She had so many questions without answers. What would life hold beyond the temple walls? How will she raise a child not to fear in such a fearful world? Will she be strong enough to make a life alone? She needed her husband's strength and assurances now more than ever.

Before the celebration of the holy day, the temple was purified with burning incense. The sweet smell faintly drifted into Mary's room evoking memories of the ritual that would be performed. As darkness engulfed the land, the sacred fires were lit at the top of the temple stairs, calling the people of Alexandria to worship. The growing crowd chanted a litany of praises, and their rhythmic voices were soothing to Mary as she progressed further into labor.

As the first golden rays of sunrise slowly fingered their way into the east wing of the temple, Mary gave birth to her first-born child. The news quickly spread throughout the temple, and as soon as she was able to, Rena returned to celebrate the new life.

When she saw the new mother and child, the high priestess knelt and kissed them both. "The great mother has blessed you with a daughter, it is wonderful."

"Would you like to hold her?"

Gently Rena lifted the baby from Mary's arms, and raising the child towards the heavens she prayed.

"O great mother, we give you thanks for the daughter you have given Mary. Bless and guide them both as they journey through life."

She held the child a while longer before returning the newborn to her mother. Reaching into her robe pocket, Rena took out a small scroll containing a prophecy that had come to her earlier that morning during the temple rituals. It was written in an ancient language, and as Rena read the sacred words, Mary gazed at her child in wonder. The scroll was then given to Mary for safekeeping.

When she was finally alone with her sleeping baby, Mary stared out the window opening, thinking of Jesus she whispered, "My Lord, what was bound on Earth is now bound in heaven."

Chapter 44

It was the day before Christmas. Mariah's due date was not for another week, but she felt huge and uncomfortable in any position. Sitting by the fireplace in the living room with her feet up, waiting for Grand, she admired the beautiful Christmas tree, recalling the fun evening they had decorating it. Staring at the fire, she was drawn back to her last Christmas with Joe. It had been a frigid winter night; she had come home from work to a dark apartment, finding only a brightly lit Christmas tree. Joe had surprised her with the tree, and they had a wonderful evening decorating it. Their first Christmas day had been full of delightful surprises, with each trying to affectionately out do the other. She took a deep breath as the tears welled up in her eyes, and the familiar lump rose in her throat.

Rachel came into the room just then, carrying a tray with tea and Christmas cookies on it. She heard the heavy breathing and became alarmed. "Are you alright?" She placed the tray on the coffee table, not taking her eyes off of her granddaughter.

"I am fine, Grand." Mariah smiled, wiping her eyes, "I was just missing Joe and feeling a little sad."

"Oh, sweetie, I am sorry, with all that's been going on I tend to forget it's your first Christmas without him. Would you like me to call John and cancel for tonight?"

"No, Grand, thank you, I enjoy being with all of you, and it won't do any good to mope around."

"If you are sure, Hon." Rachel was quiet for a moment as she poured the tea. "Did you have time to finish reading the end of the book?" she asked tentatively, not wanting to push her granddaughter.

"I most certainly did. And, I understand the importance of the story better now." She took the teacup Rachel was handing her.

Rachel poured herself a cup while agreeing the book's ending was important, yet more of a beginning then an ending.

"Mary giving birth to a baby girl was the final thing that did her in, the apostles were already upset with her for carrying on her husband's ministry. Yet, they tolerated her behavior because they believed the son she would deliver would be a replacement for Jesus." Rachel nibbled on a cookie for a moment thinking, she continued.

"They assumed Mary was shunned by their Lord because she did not have a son, so they turned their backs on the female child and denounced Mary and her ministry." Rachel choked up with emotion as she continued. "They unknowingly made a statement through their denial of her, which has reverberated down through history. The oppression of feminine power, and the resulting inequalities between women and men, is clearly connected to the church's suppression of this enlightening story."

It was Mariah who spoke now. "Grand, it all makes so much sense; especially if one was to follow the story of women worldwide from Mary's time to the present." She sipped her tea, contemplating this revelation before continuing.

"Incredibly, the persecutions and sufferings of women, which are documented, undoubtedly show those responsible down through time. I find it beyond belief that it continues today!" Both women were silent, momentarily overwhelmed by these apparent truths.

"If we look at women in the Middle East and third world countries it is still happening, and often at the hands of men in the name of religion." Quite emotional now, Mariah stopped to catch her breath. "How will this ever change?"

"We have made a little progress in the past couple centuries, but we have a very long way to go, not only to gain equality, but to liberate our less fortunate sisters in other countries." Rachel looked down at her pendant, reflecting the firelight. "That is why I have written the true story of Mary and Jesus, our ancestors. It may be a small book, but it could have a big impact." Rachel was lost in thought for a time.

"Maybe it will make the world a better place for your child."

"I do understand, Grand, and I agree with you. I feel a connection to Mary, with having been widowed myself, and I feel as though she wants her story to finally be told." Mariah had a distant look in her eyes, briefly considering her own loss.

"I had a little difficulty believing some of this at first, but the complete story makes so much sense. The facts clarify so many unjustified atrocities towards women, and finally help explain the unreasonable inequalities between the genders. There is no reason for anyone to doubt the truth of this story."

Chapter 45

Changing her clothes, Mariah stood sideways in front of the full-length mirror in her bedroom, amazed at the size of her stomach. She let her hands glide slowly from the peak of her mountainous stomach to the bottom where they disappeared from sight. She felt the baby moving, as though in response to her touch. It made her smile, "It won't be long until we meet little one."

She picked up her dress and slipped it over her head. Turning to see her reflection again, she was pleased. The emerald green velvet enhanced her glowing beauty, the v-neck showed modest cleavage, and the length would look perfect with her favorite boots. She curled her hair loosely, so it fell softly on her shoulders and away from her face, and so her sparkling chandelier earrings would show. The finishing touch was a dusting of glitter powder on her neck and chest. Examining her reflection in the full-length mirror again, she was pleased with her efforts. As she bent to pick her purse up off the bed, she had a sudden strong twinge stopping her in place. It passed after a minute, and she took a deep breath, straightening upright. She assumed it was just a false contraction, like the ones she had been experiencing quite a bit lately. Grand called to her right then, so she quickly checked her hair one more time before making her way slowly down the stairs.

There was Christmas music playing softly, and Dr. James was seated by the fire, eating a cookie. The house was filled with the marvelous aroma of the special Christmas pudding cake Rachel had made to bring to John's house for dessert.

"Mariah, you look lovely," James rose to greet her.

"It's getting difficult to feel attractive," she laughed making a gesture towards her large belly. Again, she stopped walking, as a very strong contraction hardened her body.

"You okay?"

"Yes, it's just the Braxton-Hicks contractions, but they are getting stronger."

"Yes, well your body is getting you ready for the real thing. It won't be long until we'll get to meet this little baby in person. Do you regret not finding out if it is a boy or girl?" James' curiosity was interrupted by Rachel's voice.

"James, could you come in the kitchen and carry this cake out to the car please?"

"I am on my way." He winked at Mariah, as he started towards the kitchen. She was getting a white wool coat out of the hall closet. *Thank heavens Amy let me borrow this; it is the only coat that wraps all the way around me.*

The drive to John's house took longer than usual due to poor visibility. James was forced to drive slowly, with the snow very heavy at times; even so, they all agreed it was beautiful. It filled them with Christmas spirit, and they sang carols and laughed right up to the front door.

John's house looked like a winter wonderland. White lights twinkled on all of the trees and shrubs in his yard. Two huge wreathes, with gorgeous burgundy bows edged in gold, adorned the double front doors. And a spotlight, as well as the snowfall, made them sparkle.

John answered the door wearing a Santa cap and bellowing, "Merry Christmas, Merry Christmas to all!"

This added to the already spirited mood they were in, and they exchanged greetings with laughter and hugs. John took their coats and told them to go into the living room while he hung the coats. The threesome was totally awestruck by the beauty of the nine-foot Christmas tree and the numerous decorations throughout the room, which repeated the burgundy and gold color theme.

James carried the pudding cake into the kitchen, with Rachel following behind him to put it in a warm oven. The fireplace crackled, while soft Christmas music played in the background. The room was festive, yet exquisitely decorated.

John entered the room, as they all stood there absorbing the seasonal warmth of his home. "Please, have a seat, can I get drinks for everyone?" They all took seats near the fireplace to warm up.

John left to get the drinks and quickly returned with a tray of glasses and appetizers. Rachel was the first to speak.

"John, your home looks beautiful. Everything is so festive, yet elegantly understated. If you did this decorating yourself, I am more impressed then ever."

"I love Christmas! I did supervise the decorating, with help from my groundskeeper and maid. I have waited a long time to have my own home to decorate, and I really enjoy doing it."

"Well, you have done a spectacular job, John," added James. They all nodded in agreement.

When John passed the treats around, he noticed Mariah did not take any, she had also been rather quiet.

"Mariah, how are you feeling?"

She smiled at him, "Oh, I'm fine, just tired and ready to have this baby." She was not very convincing.

"Please, tell me if I can get you anything to make you more comfortable."

"Thank you, there is one thing I would like. May I see the antique statue you recently acquired?" She smiled sheepishly, knowing this was not quite what he meant.

John hopped up. "I would be delighted to show you. Anyone else want to come?"

James and Rachel were too comfortable to move, so they passed. John helped Mariah up and held her arm, guiding her into his study. He lit the room and turned Mariah to her right. There on a pedestal was a bust size statue of a woman. She had her head slightly turned, clearly showing the classic lines of her silhouette. Her neck and shoulders were exposed, with a soft draping of material showing at the base of the figure. Her hair was pulled back and up, adorned by a few leaves on the sides, perhaps indicating a Greek style.

"Oh, John, she is breathtakingly beautiful. Do you know anything about her?"

"Not any real facts, just innuendos of who she might be from a former owner. He purchased her in Egypt, while on a business trip, and had her shipped back to the states."

"She looks so regal, like a goddess." Mariah ran her hands over the smooth marble type figure. "She is so life-like, she looks like she may speak at any moment!"

"I know. That's one of the reasons I purchased her. The workmanship is exceptional, even if the artist is unknown. But, mainly I was drawn to her because she reminds me of you." He looked down, not sure if he should have told her.

"Thank you, that is so flattering." Mariah touched the face of the goddess. "She is beautiful, and she gives this room a wonderful feeling." Mariah suddenly had an overpowering contraction and held on tightly to John's arm.

"James, James, come quickly." John's voice was filled with panic.

James was there instantly, with Rachel close behind.

They helped Mariah over to the settee, as the contraction passed. Dr. James placed his hand on her stomach. "Mariah have you been having contractions all day?"

"Yes, but only on and off, those fake ones ... a ... here comes another one." Mariah took a deep breath.

"The baby appears to have dropped considerably. We need to get you to the hospital. I'll call ahead and let them know we are coming. Looks like you are going to have a Christmas baby! Breath deep, remember your Lamaze."

Mariah looked at John, as they helped her up. "Sorry to ruin Christmas Eve."

"Are you kidding, this is wonderful!" John kissed her on the forehead.

Chapter 46

John intermittently paced nervously and sat fidgeting in the waiting room. It had only been a few hours since they took Mariah into the birthing room, but the wait seemed excruciatingly long. He was worried and just wanted everything to be all right. He was so in love with Mariah he felt like it was his wife and child in there.

Dr. James was in with Mariah to assist her doctor, and Rachel was with her for comfort. James came out briefly to tell John it wouldn't be long now. Her water had broken, and the baby had dropped more. He looked at his watch, as James disappeared behind closed doors. It was almost midnight, Christmas Day. He leaned his head back, and closed his eyes for a minute.

"John, John, wake up."

He awoke with a start, quite disoriented, not knowing where he was for a second. James stood in front of him grinning ear to ear. John jumped up.

"What's wrong?" He looked at the clock; it was one o'clock in the morning.

"Easy, John, nothing is wrong, mother and babies are fine!" James waited for a reaction.

"What? Babies?"

James laughed. "Yes, John, we were all fooled. Mariah gave birth to her son at five minutes before twelve, and her daughter at five minutes after twelve! We didn't have a clue she was having twins."

John stood there, mouth hanging open in disbelief, and then let out a cowboy howl. "Wow! That's great, really great! Is she okay? Are they all okay?" He was even acting like a new father.

James put his arm around him in a fatherly fashion.

"They are all just fine, son. You will be able to see them shortly."

Rachel came into the waiting room looking exhausted, but happy. She hugged John and then James. She sat down, and they followed.

"What a Christmas surprise this is! In all of my years I have never been so surprised. I can hardly believe there are two beautiful babies, and a girl and a boy. This is the best Christmas ever!" The nurse came in to tell them they could see Mariah now.

They all piled into her room. John went to her and kissed her on the cheek. "Merry Christmas, Mariah! Spectacular job! Two babies, two! How do you feel?"

She was laughing at how excited John was acting. "Actually, I am overwhelmed and exhausted. But they are so beautiful. It will take a bit for this to sink in and seem real!" She looked at Grand and James now. "Thank you both for being in here with me. I am so grateful for your support." Mariah started to cry.

Grand sat on the bed and hugged her. "Shhh ... now, honey, it's all right. We wouldn't have been anywhere else. We love you. Thank you for letting us be a part of this Christmas miracle."

James sat on the other side of Mariah now, and he wrapped his arms around both women. John wiped away a tear. Just then the nurses wheeled the babies back into the room, and they became the center of attention.

Chapter 47

It was early morning, but still dark out when James and Rachel reached her house. "Would you like to come in for coffee?" she asked.

"I would love to, Rach." He reached into the backseat and grabbed a pile of gifts. "These go under your tree, in case you thought Santa didn't come." She smiled, as they made their way through the snow into her house.

He went back outside to shovel the walk, while Rachel made coffee. She started the fireplace, bringing a tray with the coffee and some hot cinnamon rolls into the living room. James took off his wet things, gratefully warming himself by the fire. He lit the Christmas tree before sitting down with his coffee.

"Well, it has been quite a night." He was looking lovingly at her. "You should get some rest."

"Yes, but I am too wound up right now. I still can't believe I have two great-grandchildren!" she boasted, grinning from ear to ear.

"It's wonderful, Rachel, and I am so happy I could share the experience with you." James got up, picking up a lovely wrapped present from under the tree. He turned to her. "I would like to share all of life's experiences with you from now on." He got down on one knee. "Rachel, I have loved you for many years and promise I will love you for all the rest of our years. Will you do me the honor of becoming my wife?"

She began to cry, throwing her arms around his neck she whispered, "Yes, oh yes, James, you know I love you, and I always will." They stood hugging for some time. It was as though they had both waited all their lives for this moment in time. When they finally separated he wiped away her tears with his hanky and then dried his own face. They sat down, and he gave her the box to open.

Rachel gasped, inside was a large, brilliant emerald cut diamond set in platinum, it was breathtaking. James took it from the box and slipped onto her left hand.

"Do you like it?"

"Like it? I love it, it is the most beautiful ring I have ever seen, but that's because it's from you!" She kissed him tenderly, and they both could feel the desire within them growing. Rachel pulled away.

"James, we do need to get some sleep, so we can go back to the hospital to celebrate this joyous day with our family."

"Yes, of course, there are so many things to celebrate!" He looked at her devilishly. "I would love to stay. But, I think I should go home, so I can shower and get fresh clothes. What time shall I return for you, my love?"

"I think noon would be good. We don't want to miss too much of Christmas." Her eyes twinkled as she kissed his cheek. "I do love you, James."

"I love you more." He winked at her. "I'll be back soon. I don't know if I can sleep with all this excitement, or with being away from you." They both giggled like teenagers.

Rachel started to clean up the dishes when the sparkle from her ring caught her eye. She stopped, holding her hand at arms length, admiring her engagement ring. Between her new great-grandchildren, Mariah moving home, and her book getting ready for publication she thought she had it all, but James made her life feel complete. He was definitely her soul mate.

She turned off the lights and headed upstairs to bed, but was drawn to her study as she passed it. She put her desk lamp on, sitting down at her computer she barely noticed it was already getting light out. Deep in thought, she looked at her pendant. Since the birth of the twins something had been nagging at her, in the back of her mind. Now she knew what it was. It was the prophecy. She picked up the phone to leave her agent a message, but to her surprise Joan answered the phone.

"Joan, it's Rachel, I am sorry to disturb you. I was just going to leave you a message."

"It's fine, Hon, I was up already. Is there a problem?"

"No, not at all. I simply wanted to tell you I have decided to add a short, but important epilog to my book, it has to do with the prophecy." Rachel waited for an argument, since Joan did not like changes.

"Not a problem, if you get it to me by tomorrow."

"I'll email it to you today. I also wanted to tell you Mariah gave birth to twins last night! A girl and a boy!" Rachel was beaming with pride.

"Congrats, Hon! Everyone all right?"

"Just fine, Merry Christmas, Joan."

"Same to you, Hon, talk to you soon."

Joan didn't care how early it was, she was on the phone to Cardinal Leary immediately. She explained Rachel was adding an epilog having to do with the prophecy to her book.

"Why would she do that now?" he asked quite puzzled.

"I am not sure. I get the idea it has something to do with her granddaughter giving birth last night, but I don't know how it could be connected."

"Oh, really, boy or girl?" He tried to sound casual.

"Both, she had twins!"

"Really, how nice. Which one was born first?"

Joan thought this was a strange inquiry and wondered what he was up to. "I have no idea which baby was born first, why?"

"No reason, I was just curious." He immediately changed the subject. "I'll expect to see that epilog as soon as you receive it."

"Of course." Joan hung up curious about his behavior.

Thomas Leary opened a folder he had brought home with him. He sat there studying the translation of the prophecy he had received from the Council and thinking about the birth of the twins. Greatly concerned he reached for the phone to call the Council.

Rachel yawned and closed the computer, deep in thought about her epilog. She was quite in awe of the incredible meaning in the words of the prophecy, she had just written down. She turned her chair, gazing out at the slowly dawning Christmas Day. It had started lightly snowing again, and the world outside was blanketed in white silence, with only the sound of distant church bells tolling. She listened to the beauty of the bells, celebrating the birth of Jesus. And then slowly, like the dawning of the new day, it all became crystal clear to her.

She stood and walked to the window, gazing up at the lacey snowflakes, floating softly down, and blanketing this Christmas day in sparkling purity. Rachel, blessed herself with the sign of the cross and whispered her own pray.

"My Lord, I do not know your plans for my beautiful grandchildren. As always, Thy will be done here on Earth, as it is in heaven, but please protect our family. Dear God, please, help us! I clearly understand now, that what was bound in heaven, so long ago, is once again bound on Earth."

EPILOG

Since I began the journey of writing my book I have been blessed with a revelation. More of the Sacred Legend has unfolded before my eyes, with the first-born being a male child, for the first time in two thousand years.

This fulfills, in part, the ancient prophecy, which has been protected by the Keeper of the Knowledge and has not been revealed since ancient times.

I choose now to share this with you, the reader, so you might further understand the importance of the Legend, for the future of all of us.

Rachel

"... And when the first born of the first-born is male there will be Feminine Divine Intervention, and the balance of the feminine and masculine shall be restored throughout the lands ..."

978-0-595-49095-0
0-595-49095-6

Printed in the United States
202573BV00002B/433-525/P